Matt Gallitzin looks like any other fourteen-year old except...

that he's as small as an eleven-year old, and his eyes have the puzzled look of someone who just can't understand. He is a t.m.r.—a trainable mentally retarded adolescent.

His I.Q. is low, but his love quotient is at genius level. He adores his truck driver father, his indomitable grandmother, his high-school athlete brother—even his younger sister who is now far beyond him in accomplishment.

Then one fateful day, the strained but moderately successful system his family has worked out for coping with Matt collapses. Matt himself must find a way to pull everything together again.

ARE THERE WARNER BOOKS
YOU WANT BUT CANNOT FIND IN YOUR LOCAL STORES?

You can get any Warner Books title in print. Simply send title and retail price, plus 35¢ to cover mailing and handling costs for each book desired. New York State residents add applicable sales tax. Enclose ch or money order only, no cash please, to:

WARNER BOOKS
P.O. BOX 690
NEW YORK, N.Y. 10019

SPECIAL OLYMPICS

by
JOHN SACRET YOUNG

WARNER BOOKS

A Warner Communications Company

WARNER BOOKS EDITION

Copyright © 1978 by John Sacret Young
All rights reserved

ISBN 0-446-89718-3

Cover design by Gene Light

Warner Books, Inc., 75 Rockefeller Plaza, New York, N.Y. 10019

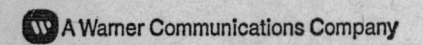

W A Warner Communications Company

Printed in the United States of America

Not associated with Warner Press, Inc. of Anderson, Indiana

First Printing: March, 1978

10 9 8 7 6 5 4 3 2 1

To
the Jeannettes

This book was possible because of the help of Deborah Dell 'Amico, Gene Newman, Ann Ruwet, Shelley Clifford, Wilmer James, Wendy Lee, Merrit Malloy, Roger Gimbel, Tina Nides, Peggy and Brian Redding, and the students and athletes of Diane Leichman School, and the Tri-Valley and Northern and Southern Orange County Special Olympians and coaches and volunteers.

PART ONE

1

A boy picked up a cardboard box that sat on the floor. It was not a particularly big box, and he looked at it and turned it over in his hands. He studied it with great seriousness and then, one by one, he tore its end flaps off until it was an open square; then he turned it again and looked through its empty middle. The boy thought a moment, and then he tried it on: it fell over his head to his neck, like an oversized crown. His face disappeared and he couldn't see. He thought about that, and then he lifted the box off and set it on the edge of the table where he sat. He looked at it again. There was clay on the table, and string and construction paper. He snatched a piece of purple paper and crumpled it up. It didn't crackle and pop like regular paper. Slightly thicker, it fought his quick hand, but he beat it to a pulp and tossed it into the box. It pleased the boy. He crumpled another and got up. He set and aimed and shot it, as if at a basketball hoop. It was a terrible shot, but it didn't faze him whatsoever. He loved the miss. He crumpled pieces of red, yellow, and orange paper, setting and shooting a rainbow of paper at the box, his enthusiasm growing.

"And Mike flips it to Dr. J.," the boy said. "And Dr. J., he shoots. Swish. The 76ers lead." Roy Burton watched the boy's last blue shot bobble from table to floor. "Matt, it's time to get ready to go," he said then. "Come on. And pick up your pile of paper basketballs."

Matthew Gallitzin leaned over the colored balls on the floor. "Swish," he said again, as he picked them up. Matt and Roy walked across the room, Matt dropping his collection of crumpled balls, stopping and picking them up, dropping another. "Blue. Green. Red. Black," he called out, wrongly identifying them.

Roy Burton stopped and looked up at the television in the upper corner of the room. Matt looked up, too: a man was running.

"That's the Olympics," Burton said.

"Olympics?" Matt said.

Burton said, "Running, jumping, rowing—the greatest events in sports."

"I run. I jump."

"Don't I know it. You certainly can't keep still. Now come on. You'll be late."

"I go home now?" Matt said.

"Right now."

"Home now right now. Yeah!" said Matt.

2

Carl Gallitzin hated the smell of the Washaminy Institution: the soupy mix of fresh paint and sweet medicines and sweat and feces. He stood just inside the main door and didn't want to go farther. He wanted to remain within whiff of outdoor air. He was a big burly man; he had a huge brow and a face cut from stone. He could sit in his truck—moving—for hours, but he couldn't keep still, now, waiting. A wheelchair went by, a doctor, and then he heard his son's running feet. White winter light winked around the boy, backlit and blotted his face, but Carl knew him: he clumped along without coordination, an awkward canter.

The boy passed Roy Burton; he could see his father and there was no mistaking him, either. No one else was so big. Matt accelerated into an attempted gallop. His awkwardness didn't bother him. He liked to run. The untied earmuffs on his hat flapped. He waved his arms in imitation. He grabbed his father's arm when he reached him, hugged it, as high as he could reach, and his father picked him up. Simply done, no sweat to it, without a word.

Carl shook Burton's hand and then stepped back to the cab of his truck. He tossed his son's duffel into the doghouse and popped him onto the high passenger seat of the cab. He shut the door and walked around to the driver's side. The rig wasn't a van or a pickup: it was a 1972 Peterbilt cab over engine tractor. It'd cost Carl $22,000 new and it'd hauled him 400,000 miles. It had 318 horsepower and, with trailer, weighed 14½ tons and could pull ten. Carl hauled himself in.

"Ready to go, Pintsize."

"I drive," said Matt.

"No. You help."

Matt reached over to his father's side, to help, to bother. He often couldn't keep still. He loved to fiddle.

"Give me some room, Pintsize," his father said. "You remember how it goes."

"Vroom. Vroom."

"Yes, but this is a diesel. First push button, pull warm-up throttle, check gauges, remember?"

"Gears."

"No, not yet. The baby has to warm."

"A truck has sixteen gears," Matt said.

"That's right. This Peterbilt does. And how many does our company's Kenworth got? How about our White?"

"A truck has sixteen gears," Matt said.

"No, not all do. Our Kenworth's got thirteen, the White has ten."

And Matt threw the gear in, and it ground. It screamed in protest.

"Hold it, hold it," Carl said. "Hands off. *No.*"

He took his son's hand away, and he engaged into first gear himself and they started to move. The racket had an enjoyable purr to Carl, to both of them.

"I've been 2200 miles in three days," Carl said, "carrying a lot of bushels. But now we got only sailboat fuel. We can really hum now and . . ."

"What's that?"

Matt never held back questions. They could come in infuriating spurts and be tough to answer. He might not even listen to the answer. He had a great, fitful, forgetful sense of curiosity. He could be quiet, too, a long time.

"What's what?"

"That," and Matt pointed.

"That's the sign that says where we are, where we're leaving."

The sign said Washaminy State Institution, and Matt watched it go by and waved at it and smiled.

"You cold?" his father asked, and turned on the heat.

The cab was decked out: There was a/c, a CB, a small fan, a radar scanner, a panoply of mirrors, and 13 gauges to watch on the dash. Matt followed one needle with a finger and imitated its jiggling rise and fall.

Carl said, "Your grandmother's delighted that you're able to come home. She . . ."

Matt reached and turned on the fan.

Carl flipped it off. "Wrong season, Matt."

Matt bounced up and down on the air cushion seat, undeterred.

His father said, "You want to shake some iron?"

"Shake some iron. Yeah!"

Still bouncing, he looked out the vistavision window at the land, the movement, as his father shifted and accelerated. He felt and was eight feet high.

3

The truck stop's tarmac had leveled everything but the large pines. Alma Rennseler Riley's father had refused to chop them. He didn't mind neon or noise. He cooked fried food, insisting on greasy. Whatever truckers needed or wanted was okay. So why the trees mattered he didn't know. He didn't really think about them, they just stayed.

Alma did think about them. They were her fingers of sanity when her marriage blew apart and she came back and began to serve her father's food. She could see them whatever the weather, however dirty the window, and bail herself partway out from despair. In her second and third year back they were still there, and she still looked, but things changed. She became a part of the place. She began to like herself again and to like truckers, especially Carl Gallitzin. At thirty-one, Alma was plain and very trim. Her uniform pressed to her, her nails were clean, and her new self-confidence gave her a glow. Her turn past thirty added to her rather than subtracted.

"You sure you want it to go," she said. "You can't sit a minute?"

She looked up from filling the plastic coffee cup. Carl Gallitzin was by the window, between her and the pines, not listening.

"Hey, I'm over here, Gallitzin. Hello. Talk to me."

"Better make it two cups," Carl said.

"How about one giant size?"

"No. Two."

"Whatever you say." She poured the second cup of hundred-mile brew and when she was done he was still looking out the window.

"I went out last night with—Marlon Brando. He's a little overweight." And then she said, "But he's great in bed."

"Umm," Carl said.

"Umm yourself. Forget the small talk. Don't be polite. Just consider me not here. As if you weren't already."

He was still at the window.

"What is it?" she said. "Are you all right?"

"I'm all right."

"The man speaks," Alma said.

Now, finally, he faced her; at last she had his attention.

"He has a face, too. How was the ride out, how's the flip-flop been?" She spoke quickly to hold him.

"So-so. Glad to be almost home."

"How's the family?" she asked. "You know someday I want to meet them, especially the Wachataw basketball legend. I have a right to, after all I've heard about him. The famous son."

"He scored 26 points against Lantenengo," he said, but she lost him again: he turned back to the window.

She knew he had humor, a tough masculine sense of kidding. She knew deeply buried, well protected, there was also gentleness. She knew his lack of language, his typical taciturnity. This was different, beyond that. She didn't know where. He had never seen her out of uniform. She had never seen him away from his rig; only here. She knew him, yet not at all.

Outside, the boy pressed his face to the gas pump, to where the numbers whirred. He held the gas cap in both hands as if it were as big as a discus. The boy, fourteen, looked eleven and much like any boy except for the smallness, and the furrows under his eyes were the shade of creosote. Even from the window Carl could sense their smudge. The gallons and the dollars and cents soared and Matt's head bobbed. Carl was 2200 miles tired and there was a tiredness beyond the miles, as he watched his retarded son.

4

Elmira Gallitzin's hands shook. They had forever, as far as Janice knew. Every day her grandmother drank tea, and Janice would watch, certain this time the jiggling hand would spill the tea. It never did. She didn't understand it.

The chicken they were preparing moved around the sink, too, as her grandmother wrestled with it. Janice was supposed to be listening and learning, but she couldn't help noticing the powerful hands. The skin had pulled back between the bones, and the knuckles jutted. The veins were cold, cold blue tubes, like lobster colons. They gnarled all together, and there was a blizzard of liver spots. What hands they were.

"Now," Elmira said, "the bird's unwired, so you reach in and pull out the giblets." And she did.

"Ooook," said Janice.

"You like the heart."

"But not all that other *stuff.*" Janice wrinkled her face in theatrical disgust and her thin-framed glasses tucked farther up her nose. She was lean and whippy, quick and stubborn; and her tightness was just beginning to turn to chrysalis: she looked fifteen, not thirteen, and she was going to break hearts.

"It's good for you. Now you make sure this is well cleaned inside, and you give the whole bird a little scrub." Elmira ran water over it. "You got the stuffing ready?"

"I've got to cut one more carrot."

"Well, get chopping. The oven's ready and I'm getting hungry, aren't you?"

"Nobody's here to eat it."

"They will be."

The front door slammed just as she said it.

"See?"

Her grandmother was so often maddeningly right. She plopped the water-polished chicken on a cutting board and turned from the sink. She called "Hello," singing the greeting, a lifetime behind it. Matt clumped in and caught her halfway across the kitchen. He hugged his grandmother's waist and she hugged him back. Janice hung back a little, holding the carrot.

"Now, where's your father?" Elmira said.

"He coming. But I come first."

"All right, then let's get you to work. No shilly-shallying."

"Work work," Matt said. "No shally-shilly."

"You better believe it," Janice said.

Matt extricated himself from his coat as his grandmother went to the pantry. He shook off the coat by shaking his whole body, especially his arms. It luffed to the floor, and he and his sister stared at it.

"I'm not picking it up," Janice said.

"Fine."

"Well, somebody's going to, and it's not going to be me. That leaves you. So do it."

"Fine."

But he didn't. He was content just looking at it. He hadn't changed at all. He was as infuriating to his sister as ever.

Elmira came back, and she told him to pick it up. He did and hung it on the hook beside his sister's, then followed his grandmother into the dining room. She had silver in her hands.

"You do that side, I'll do this. Forks to the left, knives and spoons to the right, spoons outside."

She handed him some silver and they set off on opposite sides, setting the table for five. Elmira's hands laid the silver quickly. There was a quivery moment as she put them down, and then the pieces sat in perfect parallel. Matt's work wasn't so perfect. He liked forks in strange places; he liked them together. Left, right didn't matter, upside-down didn't matter, crosswise didn't matter. But he considered each of his unique placements carefully. Janice followed behind him, correcting his work.

Elmira looked over what they had done. "That wasn't so bad. Come on, Janice. Back to stuffing our bird." Matt started to leave, too, and then didn't. He walked around the fully set table. He looked at the place settings. He looked at them and then he picked up the forks and moved them again.

5

Carl Gallitzin's size tested a standard bathtub's capacity. It was like a watery cocoon around him. He was going to buy an old, heavy, oversized tub with feet someday: he had said that for fifteen years, hadn't yet. The great white beached whale, his wife, Mary Ann, had called him, coming in and seeing him sandwiched in porcelain. She would lower the toilet seat and sit on it and set a drink on the lip of the tub and they would talk. His body would soak up Epsom, his eyes unsquint. The numbness from the miles travelled would fade away. He didn't remember what they said most of the many times. The mood, though, he did, and the easing of his muscles, and the candle she would light, and the reflection of her face.

Carl got out of the tub now and put on a clean T-shirt that his mother had monogrammed and a clean cotton flannel shirt. Then he went downstairs to carve the chicken.

"Where's Michael?" he asked.

"Basketball practice. I told him we wouldn't wait."

"No dark meat for me," said Janice.

"You've got to learn to eat both," Carl said. "When will he be home?"

"By eight. He's got to get to bed early tonight. They play York tomorrow night."

"How come I got no fork?" Carl said.

Janice passed him one of her two. "Can I go tomorrow night?"

"It's a night game, and you've got homework to do," her grandmother said.

She turned her plea upon another target. "It's *Saturday* night, Dad."

"What did you get on that last test?"

"But I wasn't even trying."

"Well, you'll be trying tomorrow night."

"I'm never allowed to do anything."

"That's tough," her grandmother said.

"Matt'll get to go see Mike. He *always* gets to go."

"He's older, and he's on vacation."

"He's always on vacation."

"That's enough of that," her grandmother said.

"Get to see Mike play," Matt said. He had been quiet, listening, watching his father carve, watching plates pass.

"He'll be home soon," Elmira said.

"I won't get to see him play, either," Carl said. "I've got to get another load to New Orleans."

"You didn't tell me that. What time?"

"Meant to. Afternoon."

"You're not getting enough rest. You never get to see your son play."

"Can't," Carl said, wishing he could.

"You're going to sleep in then." She took no nonsense from anybody, she was like a general to all of them. She was both wife and mother in many ways since Mary Ann had died.

"Won't fight that," said Carl.

"No one in this house will make a sound before noon."

"My snoring will," Carl said.

"Get to see Mike play," Matt said. He was still thinking about that and not his food, and getting more excited.

Janice made a face at her broccoli. She forked the disgusting stuff and took a stalk and snuck it onto Matt's plate. Her surreptitiousness was so successful she was disappointed. Where was the recognition for it? She pondered a moment. And then she manufactured a bright round *belch*. Matt was delighted, and belched back, a bigger one. He loved to imitate, and he had fantastic skill at belching: he was pleased with himself. Elmira was not.

"Matt, stop it."

Matt didn't. He kept them coming.

"You'll just have to leave the table then until you can stop that, young man. Go to your room."

Matt stopped, but he wasn't sure what was wrong. No one spoke. No one saved him. He got up slowly and left the table, his plate still full. Janice's plate was almost empty, certainly of broccoli, but watching her smaller older brother go, her satisfaction was bitten by second thoughts. She lost the rest of her appetite. She had won but somehow lost. She didn't understand it.

Matt turned the record player on in his room and watched the record gain speed. Just the fact that it turned fascinated him. He was still and always absorbed by what others found blase. He forgot the dinner table. He didn't feel particularly punished; he had little sense of punishment. He was happy to be home, happy to be in his room.

He turned the volume way up so it boomed. The four horsemen faded and march music began and then gave way to the next great moment in sport, his favorite. "Brasher's fallen back now," said the sportscaster recreating the moment. "It's Chatway and medical student Roger Bannister. Their time at the half was one minute 58.3. They've got a chance to do it, to break the four-minute mile. Here they come around the final turn. Dr. Roger Bannister is kicking, he's really moving, he..."

Matt sat on his made bed, next to his duffel, slapping his boots together, talking with the record, talking back to it. The stretch especially excited him. He jumped off his own bed and went to his brother's bed and bounced on it and looked at the posters above it. There was Dr. J. and there was another basketball player doing a left-handed hook. It was Mike, and Matt jumped off the second bed and started bouncing an invisible basketball. He turned and looked up at the wall again and there was a third and fourth poster, Frank Shorter running the marathon and Mike again, finishing a mile run.

Matt forgot the invisible ball and started to run in place, the record blaring, his boots clomping. He looked at the fourth blowup, and Mike was just finishing, winning the race, his arms aloft and Roger Bannister finished, he won, and Matt running in place, flashed his arms up in imitation of victory, and the four-minute mile was broken.

6

Michael Gallitzin turned on the light in the room when he came home later. The geysered contents of Matt's duffel were all over the floor, and a collection of hats topped the bureau in a formation like the trophies on his own. The second bed was in chaos, and buried somewhere in the lumps and folds was his brother. Mike had forgotten he was coming home. He was too tired to bother turning off the light again in case it might wake Matt. He dropped his clothes where he stood, and hit the bathroom. Bladder emptied, teeth brushed, he came back, crashed. The light was still on. He stuck a pillow over his head, but it still bugged him. He got up, finally, and hit the switch.

He started to throw himself back on the bed, then stopped. He hadn't heard his brother's breathing. Usually it filled the room when he was home like an asthma attack. The wheeze could keep Mike awake. It was so loud sometimes it woke Matt himself, and he had trouble sleeping anyway. Where was it? He moved toward his brother's bed, listening. Even beside it, he still couldn't hear anything. He wanted to go to bed, but where was it? He began to pick through the twist of quilts and blankets. The unwrapping wasn't easy; he ended up with a knee on the bed, his shoulder on the bed, his head nearly upside down, peering under. Mike couldn't see but he heard Matt then, the breaths as big as breaking waves under the covers. And he had been worried. There was a smell, too, and Mike jerked his head out. The kid hadn't changed at all: he had peed in his bed.

7

For years Elmira Gallitzin never woke after quarter of six. She was an early morning person, and now, for no reason, she found herself sleeping as late as seven. Irritating. She was going to have to buy an alarm. Nearly eight now, and the washer hadn't even completed Janice's flowered sheets. Whatever happened to white and to all cotton? Everything was polyesters and silly colors, even toilet paper. She had hand-washed two of Carl's shirts last night, and she got them out of the dryer. Their heat felt good on her hands, and she smelled their clean. She slapped them flat and folded them even though she was going to iron them. The rest she would hang outside wet: there was no substitute for fresh air.

The washer made a last clunk and stilled. Clunks continued nevertheless, clunk clunk, and waa-nng. She looked up and a ball dribbled by the cellar window, and boots after it. They made as much noise as the ball.

It was Matt trying to recapture the basketball. When he did, he dribbled it back toward the backboard.

"*Waa-nng,*" he said, "*Waaaaa-nng.*"

He did a good imitation of the aging, loosening rim that his last shot had hit. He had trouble dribbling, though. He knew one-handed was good, but he liked two hands, and the ball still kept getting away. Independent ball. He chased it down every time, but it never learned. He talked to himself as he played, like a commentator; the chatter warred with the cold whistling wind.

"And Mike beats his man," Matt announced, "and he sets, he shoots, swish."

He called before the ball left his hand, and it missed the rim when he did let go, his arms waving like spaghetti. The ball hit the side of the house just above the garage door where his grandmother was now standing. He chased it.

"Matt," his grandmother called as he corralled it.

He turned toward her, let the ball go. She came over to where he stood, some of the wet laundry over her shoulders.

"What are you doing up?" she said. "What are you doing out here making all this racket? You know your father's asleep. You're supposed to be on tiptoe."

"I play basketball," Matt said.

"I know, but you have to have consideration for others."

"I sorry."

"I know it."

And she bent down; she got down to his pocket size, eye to eye, person to person. She didn't show that it wasn't easy. It was cold enough so both their breaths showed.

"I'm so glad you're home," she said. "But you've got to do your best. Better than your best. Sometimes, you know—you're a pain. Sometimes all of you are pains. I don't know which one of you's worst."

"I can not play basketball?" It was a question, sort of.

"You can play. You can always play. But not now. We need to be quiet."

He accepted her verdict, brightness undiminished.

"I help with wash."

"All right, apple polisher," she laughed, "you hang these. There are clothespins on the line. I'll get the rest of the load."

She took the pile off her shoulder, and he took them deliberately and set off across the drive toward the white zags of the line. She watched him go. She was no push over, no soft grandmother, but he could almost break her down.

She went back into the house and got the shirts Carl would need. She tiptoed past his room, but the door wasn't shut. The bathroom door across the hall was; he was up. It opened and out he came.

She said, "You're supposed to be in bed."

"I know." And he walked past her into the bedroom.

She followed him and set the shirts on his bureau. She gunned open a drawer.

"You heard him," she said then, angry that he had.

She got out his heavy-collared sweater as he pulled on a faded chamois cloth shirt. "He's quiet now. You could go back."

"Doesn't matter. I don't give a rip."

"I know it's trouble sometimes . . ." her sentence faded off.

They were back to back and she held the sweater,

and suddenly she was near tears. She fought for her practiced discipline before she spoke.

"I just think it's important to have him home. Not just for a visit if we can. So he can have some real time with us, this period of his life."

Carl said, "We can't help him."

"We can love him. He is ours."

"I know. Sometimes I just wish—" He stopped, lacking articulation. "Oh, hell."

She snuck a look: he was bent over his shoes. He looked bigger than ever half-dressed, coiled and held in. He looked, also, tireder than ever.

"Maybe we could bus him over to York. Or they're supposed to open a new special section at Wachataw. Or a scholarship might open up at the private school. Maybe we could work out some way for him to commute."

"Or. Or. Maybe," he said. "Even if he did, there are no miracles. We can't save him, Mother. He is what he is."

"Maybe I'm wrong. I don't know," she said. "Doesn't he knew, Carl? He's glad to be with us, isn't he?"

"I can't get into his head," Carl said.

"We laugh together."

"How can you know what a laugh means? Who knows what's in his mind."

He had finished his shoes and he leaned now against the side frame of the window seat at the end of the room, away from her. He could see the back yard out the large window, the laundry lines, the boy botching the hanging.

"Eventually, we'll have no choice," he said.

They had had this conversation so many times,

hushed and guilty and loud and long and angry and breaking down, and then they had stopped having it at all. She left the sweater, crossed to him, touched his vast back. She let all her discipline give way.

"I just feel some moments, together, all of us together, they're possible. You want them to be," she said, crying now. "They're what we can have."

8

Matt couldn't keep his feet on it. It snaked down the drive to the street where the Peterbilt tractor was, and Matt kept falling off. He'd get his feet onto it and then they'd fall off, and he would, too. Stubborn hose, stubborn feet. He kept trying and cheating when he had to until he got to the nozzle. It was still on, and the cab had been hosed down. The vacuum was also running. Its cord, too thin to be any fun, came from the front of the house and lay like a lasso around the machine. The vacuum was halfway up onto its back legs and above was Janice's tailboard on the seat facing him. Her head and the vacuum's brush were in the doghouse.

Matt turned the vacuum off. "Want to help."

Janice refused to be bothered. "This is my job, Matt, and I don't have much time." She turned it on again, and started on the dash. She did the dials carefully and then pulled the brush off and jammed the bare end into the crack between the seat. She didn't kid around: she was going to get any dirt that dared exist. She had taken the job of cleaning it regularly for her father upon herself, and the work was important to her. She totally forgot about Matt's brief appearance and lost herself in vacuuming concentration. Only a sharp sickening screech pierced her work. She dropped the vacuum and bailed out the far side.

A car had fishtailed to a stop beside Matt, leaving rubber on the road.

"I almost hit him," said the driver. The man was both aghast and angry.

Janice didn't know him, and she grabbed her brother.

"Are you all right?"

Matt nodded, and she held him behind her protectively. He stood very close to the truck's big rear tire; he hadn't seen, he hadn't looked, he was scared. He watched his sister and the man leaning out his window.

The man said, "He didn't look at all, he just ran right out in front of me."

"Matt does not run out into streets."

"I don't know what he doesn't do, but he just did."

"Who was speeding, anyhow? Look at the rubber you left." She wasn't going to be intimidated.

"You just better keep your little brother out of the road," the man said, and hit his accelerator. He left a little more rubber.

She let the man have it then:

"You *buttnik*."

She also wanted to give him the finger for something to look at last.

"Listen, big brother, you know you're not supposed to go in the road."

Matt didn't move from the tire.

"Okay. Okay," his sister said, "you can help me

wax the front hood." She turned him and shoved him away from the wheel and around to the front of the tractor. "I'll show you what to do."

She reached up, grasped one of the two handles on the front, and gave it a heave. The entire front plate of the tractor, the cab over the engine, pitched forward toward her, like a giant visor. Janice hopped down and sidestepped the hose, picked up wax and cloth.

"You take some of this and you rub it on. See." And she did. "Little circles. See. Careful little circles. Then you take a little more, and you rub it in next to the first. Like that. I'll finish the cab."

She handed Matt the wax and the rag, and he looked them both over as she hiked herself back up to the pitched cab. Matt rubbed the rag into the wax. It was interesting. He rubbed some next to where she had. Hers was drying a milky shade, chalking. The rag was big and slippery. The wax had stained it a nicotine shade. Matt had an idea. He tossed the rag over toward the curb, forgot it, and took off his cap. He stuck its corner into the wax and used it to apply the wax. It worked. He tried little circles but they kept getting bigger and bigger. He had to run to keep up with them, smearing it in wider and wider circles. He ran around the radiator and around the headlights, as around a track, making racing noises, *rrrmmmm*.

Janice, cleaning around the pedals, came up for air and saw him.

"What are you *doing*?"
"Polishing."
"Not like that."
"Doing laps," said Matt.

"*Small* circles."

He stopped, out of breath.

"No good?"

"You're so weird. Can't you do anything right?"

She got down again and took the wax from him and then his caked hat. She snapped it back to a more natural state and stuck it on his head. Getting the rag back, she started doing the work herself. She rubbed, small, concentric, concentrated circles. She was very meticulous, and Matt came close to her, looking over her shoulder.

"You gonna do wheels, too?"

"No," said Janice.

"You gonna go to school today?"

"It's Saturday," said Janice.

"You smell."

"I—what?"

"You gonna—whattaya gonna do after this?"

"I don't know."

"Can I come?"

"Come? Come where? Who's going anywhere? Who ever gets to go anywhere?"

"When's it gonna snow?"

"I don't know."

"Where—why—what is it?"

"What is what? No more questions."

"I like snow."

"Just shut up, will ya."

"I can ride a bike."

He was still right next to her, closer than ever, and she beat her fist against the pitched hood. He was totally *non* nonplussed, totally maddening, ready to launch forth again. The hose was at her feet and she picked it up and set her thumb against its spout,

40

geysering it, and she raised it toward him ready to fire, absolutely ready, and the jetting stream collapsed. It piddled out.

She turned, looking back up the line of hose. Ten feet away her other brother was clamping the hose back upon itself, squeezing off the flow. Just showered, he wore a clean, tight T-shirt and green corduroy pants, his hair casually parted in the middle. As wide as his father, he was taller and leaner and was, as always, as far as Janice could see, casually and obnoxiously sure of himself.

She said, "The *star* is actually up."

"Come on, Matt," Mike said, "leave the maintenance woman alone."

"Mike," Matt said, turning, too.

"Let go of that," said Janice to Mike.

"Keep on truckin', washerwoman."

"I'll turn it on you as soon as you let go."

"You do and I'll pour you into the nozzle of that hose."

"Big deal, big man. Thinks I'm scared or something," Janice said, but she didn't say it loudly.

"Mumble grumble," Mike said to her mumbling grumbling. "Come on, Matt."

"I will anyway," called Janice after them, cocking the hose, but she didn't.

The two brothers followed the vacuum cord in the front way and walked down the hall and into their room.

Mike said, "How'd you get up without waking me?"

"I quiet."

"*Quiet?* Mr. Blunderbuss?" Then Mike said, "How's the state farm?"

41

Matt didn't answer.

"Not exactly the geeter with the heater, the boss with the hot sauce."

Matt still didn't answer, but he sat on the bed beside his brother. Close, so they were side by side.

Mike looked at him. "Well, say something."

"I watch you play tonight."

"Yeah, and we could lose, too," Mike said. "Get me my sneakers, will you. I've got to put in new game laces."

Matt went to the closet and brought back a small pair, his own.

Mike said, "No, chumbo. Mine. The new ones, the Converse."

Matt made a second trip as Mike got out some long orange laces from his bureau. They sat beside each other again as Mike stripped the old ones: using his middle finger he ripped them out quickly. Matt took off his coat but left his hat on. He had a too-big Boy Scout shirt on underneath, well-patched and merit-badged. He watched his brother work.

"Mine too," he said.

"Sure." Mike picked up his second sneaker, gave his brother a glance, and saw what he was wearing. "Hey, that's my shirt."

"Yeah"

Mike shook his head. "You're just lucky I'm beyond Boy Scouts, that's all. Way beyond."

Matt's boots clumped as he dropped them to the floor and began to pull out a blackened lace from his own sneaker. He pulled one end stubbornly, and it didn't want to come. He jerked it, and the shoe jumped like a puppet. He liked it; he did it again.

"No, like this," Mike said. "How many times have

we done this? How many times do I have to tell you?"

He finished ripping out his second, chut chut chut. Then he did Matt's first. Matt picked up one of the laces Mike had ripped out of his.

"Now," Mike said, "stick in a lace like this and hold up the ends until they're equal and cross under."

He started to make a bar pattern up the sneaker, the crossing beneath. He thought they looked more professional, more *bomb* that way, rather than just crisscrosses. He whisked the orange through the eyes forgetting about his brother. Only when he was done did he look over: total bollix. The kid was lousy with laces.

"How did you do that? *I give up.*"

Matt was unfazed. He kept working away, making a tangled cobweb, having a good time.

9

The last time the two teams had met had been at York, in their mausoleum of a gym, and Wachataw had lost. They always lost to York, ten times in a row, twelve, people had stopped counting. York was dropping them from their schedule. The towns had once been almost the same size; old, traditional rivals. They were now no longer even in the same league. When Wachataw came they could never fill the York gym. It always seemed huge and empty, the ceiling miles high, the fine light planks of court polished to a perfect glaze. The baskets came down by motor and locked rigidly and perfectly into place.

In contrast, the old wooden seats at Wachataw slid out right to court side. They rumbled when you walked on them and now, shoes stomping, rows of shoes stomping, they made a din. The whole tiny gym was clapping and pounding their feet. In the band box it was a cacophony. This was the final time the two teams were to meet, and Wachataw still had a chance to win.

They had led in the first quarter and then gotten cold, missing shots, turnovers. At the half they were down by ten; halfway through the third quarter they trailed by seventeen. Now, with 31 seconds left, York led 64 to 61.

In so much noise the whistle to end the time out couldn't be heard, they had to use the scoreboard buzzer. The teams broke from their huddles and fanned out, and the feet and hands of the crowd slowed a second. Matt had been pounding both his feet simultaneously.

His grandmother beside him had only learned the game during the past three years. She had to talk to Mike; he talked about little else for a third of the year. She could have done without the sweat smell that all the gyms had, but she enjoyed dropping statistics and know-how on her grandson—more turnovers, for example, almost always meant a loss, sloppy teamwork, lack of discipline. The breakfast table the morning after a game often drove Mike crazy. Her criticisms or suggestions were increasingly right.

"What will they do?" she asked Matt.

"Give the ball to Mike."

"But they need three points."

"Give the ball to Mike," Matt said.

"Yes, but—" she started to say, but it was buried. The noise rose again, chanting as well as stomping now, deafening.

Wachataw brought the ball in bounds and out of the back court. York pressed them and they moved the ball against it, quick passes, and they started to cut. Mike cut through the lane, nicking bodies, circling. His man stuck to him. Mike snapped inside a pick at the foul line, hanging his man there, and cornered on a second pick at the low post, free. The ball was there as he turned. Without any hesitation he went up: he let fly a quick, fluid, left-handed jumper from the corner. The ball dropped cleanly through.

"Swish," Matt said.

The crowd stomped louder. There were now seventeen seconds left.

York couldn't find a man free inside three seconds. The guard called time out, and aagin the teams huddled. Matt watched his brother. Everyone else's excitement made him even more excited. He wanted to be out there to help, and to show what he could do. He jumped up and down.

"Okay, coach," his grandmother said. "What now?" She knew what he would say.

York got the ball in, but the tight press panicked them. The pass went back and, hemmed in, they hurried to cross center court. They looped a pass to make it in time. Stretching, Mike got a hand on it. The deflection sent it spinning sidewise. The ball rolled loose. Mike and a York player scrambled for it, slipping. Their sneakers squelched against the wood. Even from his knees Mike kept after it. He got it, and he pitched it before he could be tied up. He didn't have time to look and see that the clock said nine seconds as he rose again. Connolly was dribbling, looking for someone open, for anything. He got it to Sarnowski. Sarnowski had no shot, had to pump it back. Connolly saw Mike cutting and let fly. Mike wasn't free, there wasn't time to get to be. He took the pass and he went up, a hand in his face. The ball made it past the defending arm, lifted and fell and danced on the rim. It didn't go in. Mike knew it had been forced: he followed his own shot and went up for the rebound. So did everybody else.

They jostled under the boards tipping it, five seconds, four seconds left, and an elbow caught Mike perfectly on the side of the head. He went down in the melee, ass smacking, and arms out and legs badly bent. Sneakers landed on one of his legs and *snap* went the ankle. Mike yelled. Whistles blew, play stopped, two seconds left.

Mike tried to hold the hurt ankle. He couldn't reach closer than to hold his knee. The pain kept him rolling from side to side. He tried again to reach it, couldn't, but Matt could. He had bolted from the stands, and he grabbed the ankle to help. That trebled the pain. Mike screamed, and Matt laughed, just an instant. He knew it was wrong, though, so he tried to just hold onto the leg. He wanted to help. Others had to pull him away to help Mike up.

It took Elmira longer to get to the floor. Two players were helping Mike out and Matt was following them, trying to stay close. They all went through the door. She hurried after them.

The halls made Matt unsure. They were dim, nightlit, the shade of butterscotch, and he was falling farther behind. They turned a corner ahead of him. He could still hear them, still hear Mike's pain. He ran to the corner, but they weren't visible either way. He didn't know which way to go; he could no longer hear them now. He made a choice, and ran down the hall.

Elmira saw him turn, but he was gone also when she got there. She went ahead as quickly as she could.

Matt went down several corridors until he saw an exit. The hospital was where hurt people went. He ran as fast as he could to the door.

The old high school had a polished wood-and-glass

revolving door. It had modern fire doors to either side, as well, but the antique mid-section revolved. Matt didn't know about revolving doors, he was swept out as some boys swept in. He rode the energy of their entrance all the way round. It was fun. He didn't get out—he went around again. The boys saw this and spun the door again. Matt went round and round. The boys laughed and Matt laughed, different kinds of laughter; Matt laughed as they laughed at him. He was trapped, and round and round they sent him, round and round he went, faster and faster. And suddenly he began to shake. His entire body tightened, like a convulsion. The boys saw it through the paddling panes of glass, and their laughter freeze-dried. They fought with the doors to stop them and get to him.

Matt saw them coming to help, but before they could, he blacked out.

10

"Hi, Grandmom," Matt said, opening his eyes.

Elmira said, "Where you been? I've been waiting for you to wake up."

"Basketball," said Matt.

"Don't you think of anything else?"

"Running, too."

"You hambone," Elmira said. "And I was all worried about you."

"Why?"

"You snuck off on me. You know you're not supposed to do that. I searched for you."

"I found a door that moved. It went around and around."

"Do you feel all right? Really?"

"I fine." The seizure and the blackout following had refreshed him. He said, "I had a fit."

"Yes."

"I was excited."

"You double hambone," his grandmother said. His straightforward innocence could glance truth and it could spear it. It could break her up, make her laugh or turn her heart.

"Let's play," Matt said.

"Play what?"

"Fifty-two pickup."

"No cards," she said. "Thank God."

"Paper-rock-scissors. I beat you." He started to throw his hands out, as if they had already begun. He was full of antics, mischief. He was full of beans, and she laughed.

"As I remember, you cheat."

"Record player?" tried Matt, not giving up.

"Wait a minute. You're supposed to get some rest and stay in here tonight. Tomorrow—record player."

"Oh."

"I'll tell you what," Elmira said, seeing his discouragement and against her better judgment. "We'll go down and see your brother. How about that?"

He was instantly out of bed and ready, and she laughed again.

They walked down the hall to Mike's room, Matt dancing ahead of her. His open-backed hospital gown lifted and luffed, a tiny spinnaker around him, and his naked backside showed like a five-year-old jumping out of a tub.

"Okay, showboat, get back her," she said. "Enough leaping around."

He let her catch up to him.

She said, "Here, take my hand."

They walked together, his hand in hers.

"How come you walk the way you do?" he asked.

"How do I walk?"

"Slow."

"We'll get out on a track sometime and see who beats who," she said.

"Grandmom," he said. "Why are you old?"

"You and your impossible questions."

Mike was hopping across his room, testing a pair of crutches. He was in a ward, a long room with other beds, both empty and occupied.

"They'll take a little getting used to," the nurse said to him. "They're adjustable, and your armpits'll get sore for a day or two. It's not easy, but it can be kind of fun."

Mike didn't look like anything could be fun. He hopped awkwardly back to his bed and set the crutches against the wall. He lay on the bed, disconsolate.

"I tried to call your father, but he could be in Kansas or Oklahoma or God knows where. I had to leave word. He'll be back then as soon as he can," Elmira said.

Mike looked at the ceiling.

"You'll be out of here first thing in the morning," she continued.

"Doesn't matter now. The season's over."

He looked at the ceiling; Matt played with the crutches.

Elmira said, "You played wonderfully."

"Yeah, and some rungehead stomps me. We could've made the state tournament, and I'll probably never walk again."

"You can always just lie here and collect bedsores."

"Sounds good."

Elmira leaned over him, "Okay, so you got your problems. You'll see someday how lucky you are. Your bones'll knit. They'll be stronger than ever. You'll be fine."

Mike doesn't answer. The ceiling holds him; he just wants to be left alone. Elmira kissed him.

"Come on, Matt," she said then.

"I stay here...?"

"This isn't home," said his grandmother. "You'll be down the hall."

"He can stay a few minutes," the nurse said. "I'll come back and get him."

Elmira looked from one brother to the other, one grandson to the other, one gifted and unhappy, one retarded and full of enthusiasm. "Okay."

Matt clapped his hands.

"But keep it down to a dull roar." She kissed him, too, and with a last look, left. The nurse went out after her.

Mike gave up his scrutiny of the ceiling in favor of the wall beside and behind his bed. He stared at it and stared at it, his leg up, and then turned: there was his brother holding on to his leg again. Matt had his hands curled about the fresh cast, like an incomplete collar of fingers, and was studying it.

"Wasn't once enough? You probably broke it," Mike said. "Now, will you get your hands off."

Matt didn't right away.

"Chumbo. Will you leave me *alone*."

Matt heard, and the collar broke—he unclasped his hands, and Mike turned back to the wall. That left the crutches still available, so Matt picked them up. They were way too big for him, but he'd seen Mike using them. He set them into his armpits, but they wouldn't fall straight to his feet. They hit way in front of him, as big as stilts for him. He tried anyway, rising up so his feet were aloft between. He was in the air, and it felt great. He made a step and a half and one crutch slipped. His balance went, and into the bed he went, into Mike.

Mike snapped, "Get out of here!"

His gloom had reached frustration and anger and almost tears.

Matt picked up the fallen crutches and set them by the bed. He backed out of the room. Mike turned back to the hopeless wall, feeling even worse.

The Wachataw team sneaked through the door at the far end of the ward, shushing each other. There were girls with them and once inside, they paraded through the lane of beds, looking for Mike. Connolly carried a basketball, and as they approached Mike he handed it to Sherrie Hensley behind him.

"Don't let him see it," he whispered.

She put it under her coat. It hid there, like an eighth month pregnancy: it wouldn't do, so she slid it around behind her back, still underneath her coat. Her coat was glossy, like a baseball pitcher's warm-up jacket.

"There he is," Connolly said. "Hey, Gallitzin."

For the third time Mike turned from the wall. He was very surprised to see them all. "What are you doing here?"

"Whattya doing lying in bed?" Connolly said. "Where's the party?"

"We're here to celebrate." Krontz, the team center, said.

"Celebrate what?"

"Celebrate your broken leg," Connolly said. "Celebrate our victory."

"It's not the whole leg, it's just the. . . ." Then he caught up. "*What?* What victory?"

"They called a foul, you know, chumbo. You didn't break your leg for nothing. Koontz almost blew it. He missed the first free throw."

"Tell us about it, Jeff," Koontz said. "Mr. forty-five Percent from the line."

"We really won?" Totally funked, Mike had trouble taking in the news.

"We went into overtime," Connolly said, "and Sarnowski made a basket for once. Two, in fact."

Sarnowski grinned. He was the team's other forward. He was dark and wiry, taller than Mike, with a wonderful set of Belmondo lips.

"Sixty-nine sixty-seven," Koontz said.

"Well, how are you," said Connolly.

Mike hitched himself up on his elbows. "I'm okay."

"It must have really hurt," one of the girls, Helen Hunt, said.

"How did you stand it?" breathed another.

"Oh," Mike said, a phoenix rising, "Easy breezy, no sweat."

"He's not a total lily, after all," Connolly said.

"Tell us about it, Jeff," said Mike. "Mr. Pass Out at the Sight of Blood."

"We practically had to bring him to the hospital because he just saw your leg," Koontz said.

"You fart knockers," said Connolly.

Sarnowski grinned.

"Jeffrey, I'm shocked," Sherrie said, still behind him.

"That'll be the day."

Helen Hunt said, "We're going to get caught if we stay here any longer. It's way after visiting hours."

"We could pull up beds and all spend the night," Connolly said. "Helen, you can be my personal nurse. Keep my"—he cleared his throat—"sheets warm."

"Fat chance," said Koontz.

"She can speak for herself." Sherrie said.

"I certainly can," Helen said. "And do."

"You said it," said Koontz. *"You said it."*

"I guess we'd better get out of here," Connolly said.

Mike said, "Thanks for coming."

They all turned and started to go, and then Connolly turned back. "Oh. We brought something for you. This...ah...."

And Sherrie stepped clear and unsnapped her glossy coat. She brought out the basketball and held it out to Mike.

"—game ball," said Connolly.

They all laughed and Sarnowski grinned and Mike was completely overwhelmed. He kept turning it over in his hands after they left, feeling the seams. The gift grew bigger and bigger to him. He got up and got a crutch under one arm, the ball under the other. Flaunting them, he crutched down the hall. He was a man of status now and full of himself.

"Hey, Matt," he said, reaching his brother's ward, ready to apologize. "See what the guys gave me. Hey, Matt." His voice changed then. *"Matt?"*

There was feverish activity inside the door. The resident and two nurses were trying to hold Matt down. But the strength of his shaking made them shake, too. He was having another seizure.

11

Doctor Herbert Wedemeyer made his hands pinken. He willed them to warm, bio-feedback. He stared at them and they shook a little from his concentration. A folder was in front of him waiting for the parents of its contents to arrive. He had seen many, many, many folders, facts but not antidotes. He believed in facts and not antidotes. It was a difficult, wearing belief: people wanted them, he had wanted them himself. For years he had been a consulting diagnostician, and he had learned to lay way back. He did now, waiting, his hands up above a hundred degrees. When the knock came, he let his hands cool, before getting up and answering the door.

He introduced himself and then said to Elmira and Carl Gallitzin, "Doctor Dahew asked me to look over your son's, your grandson's, chart and background to help make a recommendation. He's just come home from the state institution for a visit. How long has he been there?"

"Most of his life," Carl said. "Since his mother died."

"We were hoping this time it might be more than a visit," Elmira said.

"He's been home how long?"

"Three days. Three and a half days," Elmira said.

"And he's had two seizures?"

"Yes," Elmira said.

Wedemeyer was quick with the questions, patient with the answers. He gave them time, watching them through his gold-framed glasses. His pride was in his objectivity. He absorbed information; he didn't state opinions. He let them form out of the answers themselves.

"He has an I.Q., it says here, of 49."

"Or 56 or 64. It's been measured so many times and it never comes out the same."

Wedemeyer flipped some pages, checking; he nodded. "He's had *grand mals* before?"

"Many when he was *really* little. But less and less, recently," Elmira said.

Wedemeyer flipped some more pages. "There's not a problem with his chromosomes, no major injury to the brain. It's not acquired." Then he said, "His retardation is idiopathic?"

"Yes," Carl said. "We don't know why." He knew the language: there had been so many of these conversations for him, too.

"Do you think Washaminy is helping him?"

Carl said, "It seems to be all right."

Elmira looked at Carl and then back at the Doctor. Her glance wavered only a second. Wedemeyer watched; he had a very plain, inclusive stare.

"He's fourteen," he said. "Is he getting big, is that a problem?"

"He's small," Elmira said. "But both his father and his brother grew late."

Wedemeyer said, "In puberty seizures can accelerate.

It's not uncommon. The danger isn't so much, we can usually control them medically, but it is a factor. I can't make a decision for you. I can only offer you my best counsel. There are many things to consider. Maybe you've done so already." He watched them. "He's not really a child any more. Shaving, for example. He's always going to need some supervision. There are sexual matters. Things have changed. Sterilization isn't common among boys any more. It can be a problem area, though, depending." He let the sentence lie—he watched them. "What happens if either of you—dies?"

"Carl Gallitzin may die. I'm never going to die." Elmira said.

She knew they were both watching her now. She was trying to make light but her constraint caught her, her sense of loss. The inevitability was like evidence mounting, and it sneaked through her levity despite her best fight.

"Have you made provisions in your wills as to how he'll be taken care of?" Wedemeyer said. "Just in case?"

"We love him," Elmira said then, breaking down, her fight abandoned. Her crying made Wedemeyer look down at his paled hands. They shook a little, not bio-feedback. "Yes, I can see that," he said, after some time.

PART TWO

12

Scenery rolled by a window: winter trees and rolling hills and jags of rock blasted away to permit a highway.

"Tree. Mountain. Rock. Big road," Matt said.

"Turnpike," Elmira corrected.

Matt leaned forward beside Elmira, the better to look out. "Big road," he said.

He continued to look out; his grandmother was quiet; his father drove. Carl said then, "Matt, you're going to be a man soon, and I'd like to tell you things. Difficult. I'm no talker. Neither are you." Carl tried to cut his words into simple blocks. In turmoil, subjects sometimes went, contractions sometimes went. For very different reasons he and Matt then almost shared a way of speech.

"We want the best for you, Pintsize. Difficult to know what it is. We're trying and not going to stop. You hear me?"

His son didn't answer, he just watched his father drive, loved to watch.

"Say something."

"A truck has sixteen gears."

"Yeah," Carl said. "This one does."

"Or thirteen, or ten."

A piece of learning had lodged, and Carl turned over inside. "Hell, I don't know."

They turned off the highway in the Peterbilt cab and passed the Washaminy sign and coasted up the hill, braking, until they reached the main door. Carl reached over into the doghouse and got Matt's duffel. Matt climbed down after his grandmother hugged him. With his bag and with his father he went up the walk, and once he turned all the way around to wave, not wanting to go. His father took him as far as the door, not wanting to leave him now that they were here.

13

Elmira Gallitzin fell asleep when they got back home. She lay on her chaise and threw an afghan half over herself. She closed her eyes and tried again to convince herself of what she didn't believe, that what they were doing was best. She expected that she would have to struggle to calm down, but the tiredness was greater than that, and she went right to sleep.

In it she swam in and out of dream and memory. She was in the wheat field as a child in Nebraska and she could hear the dog. He wanted to find her, he was lousy at sniffing, disproving that supposed trait, the dog was growling, barking and hoping she would appear, and she lay looking up through the wheat at the sky. Her body flattened a section of the wheat, a humanoid shape, and the rest of the field whispered to her. Her perspective was like looking up at tall buildings. Just that sense, and the whispering turned wind and there were buildings. The wheat went to cobblestone. She was talking to the gentle policeman the blustery night she had spent in jail before Sacco and Vanzetti had been executed. The firebrand she encouraged in herself sought to antagonize him. He wouldn't accept any such cubbyhole, and she had never known whether the two men were innocent or guilty, only believed there was wrong. Maybe then she discovered the kind of fire that was within herself. She liked people. They had so many stories, the moments and aims of their lives. She became a math teacher in New York and a New Dealer. Math had a steady logic that pleased her—she truly wasn't a radical—and there was the instant when a concept would seize a student. The letters and symbols would suddenly shake out into a simple coherence. She still got to see that pop of surprise, as clear as a chuckle in Janice, who was a quick, quick student.

Elmira had been ready to teach all her life until she met Phil. He came to New York to represent coalminers and drove over a telephone pole in front of her school. He was a big, funny, brusque, loving, violent, honorable man. Cancer, when it came, subtracted the passionate adjectives of him one by one. For a long time she couldn't remember him except as a shredding invalid. She could not remember the man. She couldn't hack back through the ugly others. Until she had a dream of him in which he was the infuriating coalminer in a stiff shirt and a new suit. The shirt disappeared somewhere, she supposed, but the tweed coat from the suit he wore until he died. They were climbing Mt. Adams, silly to do in a suit, but that was the dream, and she had no trouble again. He would burst upon her at any point from the twenty-two years, often the most insignificant moments. She didn't remember him in bed—though she remembered what she had felt—but she remembered his noises in the bathroom. She remembered the way his arm followed through throwing a football to his son. She remembered the light in his face in a car on a day where she could not remember anything else. She could always hear this voice. She remembered, too, moments together: they weren't visual so much as textual, the taffy or togetherness. This was what hurt her now, even as she woke. Sleep hadn't put away Matt's separation. She was going to have to deal with it day by day. The clock ticked.

Carl would bury himself in his work. His work, like sleep, wouldn't really help now, she knew. Janice would be home soon, and then Mike. She could work on her preserves, make some aspic or ice cream. Tomorrow she had a church meeting, she had a Dorothy L. Sayers to finish re-reading, and a book about the last presidential campaign. She still loved current events; dreams and memories were fine but she loved the present. She turned on the kettle for tea and went outside and cleared the snow that had so softly, softly begun to fall.

14

In the room there were many cots and many windows with wire in them. The beds had rubber bed pads and the sheets tended to slide into a crumple in their middle. The blankets on the bed were army gray and green. It was a beige room, while other rooms were pink or yellow. The linoleum floors in every room were exactly the same. They shined briefly after Lysol, then dirtied quickly again. Tiny lockers, which served as closets, squatted between the cots. Smooth stucco finished the heavy concrete walls, and they kept heat and smells in. Stuffed animals perched on many beds during the day.

Boys slept in the room, and in the others girls slept. There were also smaller rooms—for two, and private ones—and there were hospital-like rooms where some lived incontinently in overlarge bassinets.

In this particular beige room there was a boy who couldn't really see. His eyes couldn't coordinate and his black frames held lenses, like Steuben. He had brain damage. He held his head askew, his mouth had an unusual twist, and his hand could bend to his wrist without effort. There was another boy who couldn't close his mouth. He was a Downs-Syndrome child, and his tongue seemed huge while his fingers short. He was wide and squat, and his face had the look of pink putty just hardening. There was a boy who had hardly a head, a microcephalic, who did a sort of rocking dance when he walked because his feet weren't quite whole. He was quite timid but a happy boy. Another boy had lumps of pimple, stacks of acne, and one gay tooth the shade of chewing tobacco. He could talk dirty. There was a boy who bent. He could not stand straight and he could not move freely. His joints all seemed arthritically tied. Changing his shirt was a problem. There was also a doughy boy who didn't like to move. He liked to stay in whatever position he was in, cramped or comfortable. Another boy was a twitterer. He turned forever a piece of foil between his fingers. There was a boy who liked to laugh. He wore a head brace and glasses, too, and would concentrate for long periods of time on a single sight and laugh. There was a boy who masturbated very often. One boy didn't have an incomplete arm and liked to grab and hold on with the other. His one good arm was very strong and demanding. He wanted attention, but getting it didn't appease him. There was a boy who looked absolutely normal. He had the shyest grin; he was very slow. There were many boys, odd and very odd, quiet and noisy, bad and good.

And there was Matt.

15

Alma Riley saw him coming, through the window. She was always surprised how big he was. The rig blocked the pines and Carl's wideness seemed to block both. The way he walked she knew he was feeling good.

"Well, tell me about it," she said, before he could sit down, before cup was even on saucer.

"Tell you about what?"

"You don't grin. You're not a grinner. But you're pleased. You roll when you walk when you are."

"Where did you come from?"

"I came from here and I went away and was never coming back and I came back and it was better than I thought. Not so bad, really. I can stand it."

"You like to talk."

"I do like to talk, but I don't talk that much. I can be quiet."

"Noticed that, too," Carl said.

"What else have you noticed?"

"Not much."

"I'm embarrassing you."

"Not so."

Alma said, "I like you."

"What?"

"I'm embarrassing you now, guy. See."

"Cut it out."

He knew he was different here than anywhere else. He was always tired, he liked the coffee, the sense of clean grease, the sit of her uniform, the cot in the back for a nap if he needed it. He hadn't thought about it more than that. He hadn't realized how much she had opened him up. His talk had only been short bursts, tall truths of the road and his eldest son, his biggest prides. The deeper part was his easy feeling, the looking forward to coming. He was broaching an intimacy with her, and he hadn't done that in twelve years.

"I still say you're pleased," Alma said.

"Am I going to get coffee or not?"

"An answer and you got it."

"I've been drinking it day and night. Sure as hell don't really need it. Should give it up, anyway."

"Who do you think's going to win this game," she said, "me or you."

"What game? I don't know what you're talking about."

"I know who is, I am," she said. "Mostly because you're having so much fun and you *want* to tell."

"Alma," Carl said.

The softness in his voice shivered her, and she turned back. "What?"

"Coffee!"

Then he told her and then she poured. He had just made the biggest delivery in his little company's history. Coming Monday, he was going to start leasing truck number four. The satisfaction was of years, not minutes, that high.

"The first truck we had," he said, remembering, "was a garbage truck. Had been. We banged it back into a working rattletrap. I hauled tons in that mother before it died. Even after I could afford my first Mack it hung around. It had a hell of a diesel in it; everything fell apart but that baby. It took my wife to the hospital for the delivery of our second son. It had been sitting there so long unused by then it shouldn't have even started. It did. It purred. Well, not purred—but we made it alive."

"You've never said a word to me about your second son." Alma said.

"I got rid of it shortly after that. I hated it by then. I blamed it. I blamed anything and everything I could find," he said. "Don't do that any more. Don't do it now, I hope."

He had heard her and was answering. She didn't understand him but she saw the sea change: he lost the gratification of this trip; his celebration broke down. The fourteen-year-old trap door sprang as quickly as brand-new.

They had stepped out of the safety of small talk, and he backed off. He didn't like himself for it, but he couldn't find a way back. He left without mending. Her bumping into his secrets, his need for them, hurt her. She didn't want to bump again, and she didn't want to present the check. She stalled until she could no longer. She hated it lying there, she hated the coins lying then on top of it. The unpocketed jumble had such finitude.

Driving again, Cary went through the sixteen gears. He ground them against the box. He moved it out, shook some iron. The weather turned to sleet and then to rain—winter's end. The road sizzled dangerously. He needed the danger and the windshield wipers and the great white noise of the diesel to ease a fraction of his mind.

16

Buh wop buh wop buh wop
Matt liked to do them.
Buh-wop buh-wop buh-wop
No one else liked to do them, and it was all he liked to do.
Buh wop buh wop buh wop

The rest of the day he pasted construction paper, pounding pieces into patterns. Sometimes he liked the patterns, colored popcorn, snowflakes, raggedy stamps. They played music but never basketball games. He called his own sometimes and was told to shut up. A tour had come through one day while he was commentating. The mentally retarded people had quick open antennae, while visitors were tight and too bright. One m.r. snatched a woman's glasses, and she tried to saccharine her trepidation, her fear. He saw right into the heart of it and began to shout. The tour grew absolutely still. A lot of shouting and Matt lost track of his game. The glasses flew to the floor beside him and he picked them up. He jiggled their wounded arm. They looked like Janice's.

Buh wop buh wop buh wop

He had few friends. Larry and Mary Ellen held each other a lot and Merv was an ass pain. No one liked basketball the way he did. They all liked to move slow, and he liked to move quick. He tried slowing down. He liked to imitate so he imitated that and gradually found a sedentary middle. It was fun for a while, but it didn't make him happy. He grew quieter. He got cold more and wore many clothes, floppy layers like a clown. And he cleaned toilets.

Buh wop buh wop buh wop

You had to scrub that cold shiny surface stone and sneak up in the corners where rust grew and clean around the edges and the floor from where those who shot from way back missed. And there were fierce smells, and the flush. He loved the flush. He loved the noise and the energy and the movement. *Whushhhh.*

That and the plumber's helper, he played that on the floor. It sucked. He played it in front of him, he played it between his legs, he played it to the sides, different sounds, different sucks. Sometimes the toilets didn't get so clean, but he played and plunged:

Buh wop buh wop buh wop

17

"I will never go all the way," Janice said.

Barry said, "You know what Tania says. She says she has. She says she's ready to tell me all about what it's really like."

"She's six months older than you and she thinks she's Sally Sorethroat."

Barry couldn't stop herself from giggling. "She probably is."

"She's a total *boofer*."

"Oh, Janice," Barry said. "So gross."

"No nasty, raspy, bull pukey, caca brain is going to get me. They're all really spiders anyway."

Barry said, "Zachary, too?"

"Well, he's maybe, sort of, kind of, a third, decent."

"That's only because he's smarter than you in math."

"No one's smarter than me in math."

"Such modesty," said Barry. "I heard he likes Cynthia."

"He would with those crotch crawlers she wears."

"It's probably because she's a cheerleader."

"Those stucker uppers." Janice said. "I'd never want to be one."

"That's why you tried out."

"So. So did you."

"I'm way too tall," Barry said. "When I try to cartwheel I'm a building falling over."

Nearly six feet and gangly still, she hunched herself in hopes of shrinking; she didn't realize the power in her size, or her handsomeness. Barry's height didn't mean a thing to Janice, a reason for their new friendship.

"Big deal. Who wants to do them, anyway?"

"You do," Barry said. "What are you looking for, anyway?"

They were in Mike and Matt's room and Janice had searched the closet and Matt's bureau and was on her way to his bed. Barry checked every place she checked after her.

"My brother used to have a Wonder Woman poster before he put these others up." She pointed at the two of Mike, and Dr. J. and Frank Shorter, then she flopped on the bed. Barry flopped after her.

"Won't your brother notice if you swipe it?"

"He doesn't live with us now."

"But your older brother, will he notice?"

They both lay prone, searching with their hands behind the bed by the wall.

"He won't care. He's too busy being a star," Janice said. "Aha!"

She plucked out the furled poster.

"What about your grandmother?" Barry asked.

"Not if I hurry. I'll say he gave it to me."

She bounced off the bed and dashed out of the room leaving Barry still exploring.

There was a hammer on the bed in her room. She picked it up and balanced herself precariously on the headboard. She unrolled Wonder Woman, and it rolled right back up. She held part down with an elbow and tried to center it. Perfection was impossible, so she just set it, lined up a tack and hit it.

And the sound of the record player began very loudly. Matt's record player. There was the blare of march music and then the next great moment in sports, Don Newcombe's perfect game. Janice's elbow came up, the Wonder Woman poster rolled up again, and, after a moment, Janice got down off the headboard.

She walked back to the other room with the furled poster. She felt things she didn't want to feel. She felt caught in the act, and she felt frustrated, and angry, and ashamed.

"How come you had to turn that on?" she said.

18

The door opened and Matt came into the room, half-dragging his duffel. Roy Burton came in after him and sat on the solitary bed beside him.

"You'll like it here, Matt. You'll be happier. We have three groups, "C", "B", and "A". "A" group has privacy and certain privileges. You're well-behaved and you've earned it."

"Basketball?" Matt asked.

"No, no basketball, Matt. We have arts and crafts and a store and many other activities. They're just as good. We'll come up with others, too."

"Running?" Matt asked.

"We'll see. We want to help." Burton said then, "Is there something bugging you?"

Matt didn't answer; he stared passively at his packed duffel. He didn't look up until after Roy Burton had left and the door had closed and locked.

He looked around, then, and walked to the walls. He touched them, he tapped them, *tap tap tap*. No hollowness whatsoever. He ran his fingers along them. He felt them from corner to corner, every inch. They were so thick they were completely soundless.

After his circle, he walked back and reached into his duffel and pulled out his hat. He walked to the one small window and looked through the bars at the last light. He stood looking, as quiet as the room. A slight sound started then and it didn't stop, a grating, like short strokes of a nail on a blackboard. He was grinding his teeth.

19

Sherrie Hensley leaned over toward Mike from beside his foot. The foot was on the school library table where he was trying to read.

"When am I going to get to sign your latest cast?" She asked.

"Anytime you want."

She inspected the many scrawls: "I wanted to be first, Michael. And now there's no room."

He moved to try to get a better look; not easy to do.

"Don't you ever get tired lugging it around?" She asked.

"Nah. This new one is light plastic stuff."

She traced her pen over Helen Hunt's gigantic scrawl. She did it in such a way that he felt he could feel it.

She wore Danskins and an unzipped, silver lamé, Porsche jacket, and she was very lithe and fully arrived; its lava poured over her conservative upbringing.

He said, "It itches sometimes."

"Where?"

"Inside."

"Let me see."

Sherrie looked and then slid the back end of her Bic between leg and cast, tickling the itch. It was a sensual act: his leg was aware of it, it wanted to jump. So was he and so was she.

She offered him a ride home, but on the way he had her stop beside the road within sight of the football field and track around it. He opened the door and managed to get out of her white Firebird. He braced himself in the wedge made by the door and roof and reached back in for his crutches.

Sherrie was around the car from the driver's side before he had them. "Forget them. Here." She offered her shoulder.

He hesitated and then put an arm around her, using her weight for support. They started to hobble together toward the track. The grass was pale, the beginnings of spring; the smell and softness of it was in the air. They crossed the cinder and stumbled on the far side and fell, tangling legs and lamé crinkling and laughter.

Both stumble and fall were not really mandatory.

"You did that on purpose, Michael." Sherrie said, extending his name—and what the crackery in her voice could do with that extension. She iced it with disparagement and, as well, made it the only name in the universe.

"Did what?"

"You're terrible."

"I think I broke the other ankle."

"I hope so," Sherrie said.

"I hope—the first one's ready for track. It won't

be long now. They should be working on it right now. It's in *bad* shape."

"I give you a ride in my Firebird and do somersaults with you and you talk about track."

"I love track. I love running. Basketball I really like, but it's not like track."

"Yeah, it doesn't smell as bad."

"What do you want me to talk about? The fact that I'm going bald?"

That gave her the chance to negotiate the inches between them and inspect the fallout.

"El Baldo," she said.

"My life is so *dogged*," he said.

"Your life is. My father won't let me out past eleven, and my mother thinks I'm ten."

Sherrie was a doctor's daughter, the only child for ten years. Her father was successful and her mother was a careful, socially acceptable alcoholic. Her fine looks never recovered from Sherrie's birth. Her body wasn't strong, and she wasn't happy with a child. The guilt of that ate at her and she tried to bury it in sweetness and rigidity. She started to let herself go. Sherrie was a gorgeous child and she learned how to get things. She teased. When her brother came and when her body changed she had to change her teasing. The rules were the same, the weapons different. Her practice and her weapons were very good; it was what she knew best. She could win almost anything she wanted. She didn't understand, though, why the victories didn't satisfy her.

"My family is totally messed up and my little brother—" she stopped: "Hey, where'd you go?"

"Nowhere," Mike said.

"I'll bet yours isn't half as rotten!"

"Nah. My mother's dead. My brother's a retardo." He tossed off the facts flippantly, a kind of cover.

They set Sherrie back about six feet.

And his own flippancy bit Mike back: it backed him up over the sore troubled spots, and he tried to get into them.

"My mother had a blood disease. I don't remember her very well. I remember she was skinny, she had big cheekbones. She smelled good sometimes and she smelled sick sometimes. I remember the sound of her voice saying my name. I remember she was smiling the last time I saw her. But my memory of her isn't like the pictures of her around our house. She doesn't look skinny or bony. I get confused between them. I was pretty young. I don't know if she was ever totally well after my brother came. He was born—that way. He's all energy but no smarts. He's a retardo." Saying it again didn't feel any better than the first time. "He can do some things, I guess. He's been home a couple of times since my mother died, but it never seems to work out . . . he's a good kid . . . he's in an institution again . . . right now . . ."

They lay a while sucking blades of the fresh grass. Mike needed to say more, but he didn't know how. The things he felt wouldn't simplify enough. They made him hurt and they found release only when she said his name. For the afternoon her crackery dropped the artifice and not the extension of his name. It coiled him into wanting, and the wanting would simplify beyond where it came from and what it meant. He needed it to; and her lips he could get.

20

The world spun. Matt held onto a pole and swung around it and the world spun. There went the trees and the buildings and the rubber seesaws and the merry-go-round and Roy Burton and the other kids, and around he went again. One thing that floated by was the loading platform behind the dining room. He swung around again and there it was again: all kinds of packing crates were there.

Matt stopped his turn and let go of the pole. He dribbled his invisible basketball over to the crates and reconnoitered them, forgetting the basketball. One was a big empty carton on its side. He walked around it; it was huge, as big as he was, bigger. He came back to the front and walked into it, exploring. All the way in, he scaled the sides—the actual bottom—and the carton tipped. It hesitated at its focal point, unsure, and then his moving weight carried it upright. He was now inside four walls. He looked around at corrugated cardboard.

"Hey," he yelled. "Hey!"

No answer, so he punched the cardboard. He

punched it then as hard as he could. The cardboard didn't care about his punches; in fact, it hurt him.

"Hey," he yelled, "got to get out of here."

He was angry and mad and furious, and he kept punching. The box wasn't going to beat him. He punched, he hit, he slapped, he pulled at the wood framing. It didn't care.

"Don't want to be here," he said. "Don't want to be here. Gettagottaheregottagettaandgohome."

His words washed out: they became tight frantic gurgles. At last he tired of yelling, he tired of hitting. His arms fluttered, a silent flapping. They stopped and he was still. He was absolutely still. The box had beaten him.

That was how Roy Burton found him.

21

"I'm Joanne Levine," the woman said, pronouncing the "i" in her last name long. "The special school's clinical psychologist. You were on our waiting list and with the new federal law, 94-142, we can't have a waiting list any more. Which is good. Everyone has a right to placement. But it's going to drive us crazy for space, and we've got to find and wire some more manpower." She corrected herself, "Person power. Which takes time. But are you still interested in having your child come here?"

"Yes," said Elmira, quickly.

"We have profoundly retarded here," Joanne Levine continued, "and we have borderline educable. I.Q., per se, doesn't help us. The factors for admission, now that space is no longer a consideration, are more based on social skill and motor skill than on a number. What we do is we meet and interview the student, and we ask you some questions."

Carl interrupted her. "He's fourteen and in those fourteen years we've talked to a hundred doctors, Doctor Dahew, Doctor Matthews, Doctor Wedemeyer, Doctor—"

Joanne Levine interrupted back: "These aren't medical questions. They're just . . . simple . . . questions."

"All right," said Carl. "Go ahead."

"Can Matthew talk?"

"Of course," Carl said.

"Can he make sentences?"

"Yes," Carl said.

She asked her questions with a quick individual weight. "Is he toilet trained?"

"Yes," Carl said.

Elmira said, "Sometimes at night he wets."

"Can he brush his teeth?"

"Yes," Carl said, a little more slowly.

"Can he tie his shoes?"

". . . Yes."

"No," Elmira said.

"Can he take out the garbage?"

". . . No."

"Can he make a bed?"

Carl didn't answer.

"No," Elmira said.

"Can he ride a bike?"

"Tricycle," Carl said. It barely came out.

"Two-wheel?"

Carl's head fell. The "simple" questions, the ordinary things had become a painful litany. More than any long medical terms they were Matt's sealed fate. And there was shame with the pain.

"No," Elmira said.

"Can he count change?"

"No," Elmira said.

"Could he make a transaction at a store?"

"No."

"Can he read at all?"

". . . No." The questions had even gotten to her.

Joanne Levine said then, "This is a test he can flunk. If he had a perfect score you wouldn't be here; we couldn't take him."

ing what the hell was he doing, so he never got to decide. Roy Burton was the first one to reach the truck to ask him if he was all right.

"I fine," Matt said.

23

Elmira Gallitzin marched down the department store floor to the foundations department. Janice wagged along behind her.

"We need some help," Elmira said to a saleslady.

"Yes, ma'am."

Janice said, "I don't need one."

"You certainly do. You've been putting this off long enough."

"None of my friends wear them."

"That's nonsense," Elmira said. "You just want to show off."

Janice wore a plain, linen-like shirt with button-down pockets, her figure erupting behind them.

"I don't know what you mean."

"Such foolishness," Elmira said. "It's fine if you have small breasts, and I know it's modern, but yours aren't going to be small."

The saleslady was caught between all this.

Elmira said to her, "We would like to fit this young lady with some bras."

"Yes, ma'am."

Elmira said to Janice, "Active, athletic girls need firm support."

"Oh, Grandmom."

Elmira was an alive, opinionated, stern, commanding woman, and she wasn't intimidated by the intimacy of the event. All of Janice's thirteen-year-old contradictory emotions were revved up, though. She was all up and down about the whole operation; she was excited, and askance—at least trying to be.

"Janice, you're a young woman right now. Girls grow up faster than boys. Always true. But you even more so because you have to, because of your mother, because if Matt does come home and go to the special school, because . . ." She was still hoping against hope. She started again, "I'm talking about the whole kit and kaboodle of you."

"What if I don't want to grow up?"

"Try and stop it."

"I got my rights," said Janice. "I'm the youngest."

"Yes," Elmira said, "but I also see the stuff you're sneaking onto your eyelids."

"I don't know what you mean."

"Well, don't blink, then," Elmira said.

Janice did despite herself. There it was, all right.

"I'll fool you yet," she said.

"But you don't need to," her grandmother said, gently.

There were pockets of explosion and there was love between the two women, old and young, as if there wasn't a generation skip between them. And Elmira turned her to the oval mirror on the glass counter. Both their faces appeared in the oval, as if they were posed for a cameo.

"Now take a look at yourself," Elmira said. "For

real. That's a young woman. It's a face that can wear eyeshadow, but does it need to?"

Janice mocked her features. She slapsticked herself, but the mirror caught her then. The grimaces gave way, her face reassumed itself, it relaxed. The bones showed, the young showed and the young woman showed, links to the steady lined face of her grandmother behind. Elmira put her hands on Janice's shoulders.

"It's a lovely face," she said. "Now go get yourself fitted."

Looking back once, Janice went to the fitting room, where the saleslady made her take off her shirt. She did have breasts; there was no question about it. Zachary called all breasts by fruit names. Hers were between lemons and peaches. Zachary would have liked to get his hands on them. Breasts interested him almost as much as mathematics. The saleslady had many bras. Some were white and had bones and others were flesh-colored and her breasts were held by those but they showed as if not covered at all. One for fun was black and clasped in front. Just the feel of them on was an experience. They almost tickled, the gauzy gossamer, the noisy nylon, the sandpapery spandex, whatever the stuff was.

When Janice had first menstruated she had a similar panoply of emotions. She knew all about it second and third hand, yet wasn't at all prepared for it first hand. Her grandmother also took care of that without any nonsense. Simply, directly, she explained what it was and dealt with the blood and the pain; and the pleasure and greater pain and greater love that would come eventually when an egg would be fertilized.

After Janice disappeared Elmira turned and bumped

a hat on the counter next to the foundations. There were many hats there and a larger three-sided mirror. Elmira repoised the one hat and the whole array caught her eye. She picked one up and tried it on in the mirrors. This stern, frank woman looked at herself and then tried a second and a third. In their fashion, in the facets of the mirrors, she glimpsed her youth and her old age, many things. She smiled at herself, *such foolishness,* took off the last, and took a last bare look, and she started to turn away, and it was then she collapsed.

She was dead before she hit the floor, the way she would want to go.

24

Mike walked with Roy Burton to Matt's room. Cast gone, he used just a cane now.

Burton said, "He's not happy, he tried to run away. We don't understand what he's going through. He had all this energy, and now he just sits. Sometimes he's silent and sometimes he talks to himself."

The door to Matt's room had two square holes in it. They were oddly placed, high and low, so he could see out of one and adults could see in the other. Mike looked through the high one.

All the furniture in the room was shoved to the far window and Matt sat on the bed, looking out. He rocked slightly. His feet swung off the end of the bed. Mike could just hear his voice through the door.

"It's Chatcan and Medical Bannister. Time at half one minute fifty-eight point three. They got chance to do it, four-minute mile. Here they come around final turn. Doctor Roger kicking. He really moving. He coming to wire. And wait. Here come Mike Gallitzin after him. He catching him— He—"

Mike knew the record, he had heard it endlessly.

He had wanted to break it so he would never have to hear it again so loud! But he had no idea Matt could memorize it. And the mention of his own name surprised and stopped him and reached down into that part of him where thoughts and feelings touched and merged.

"And winner is," Matt said, and then he stopped.

He said no more. His legs still swung. The chute of light from the window washed him.

Mike walked into the room. Matt turned and saw him and then even his legs stopped.

"I'm taking you home, Matt," Mike said.

PART THREE

25

Carl Gallitzin bent his big body to the ground. He knelt and then he lay flat. From beside him he took a silver box, not much bigger than a cigarette holder for a coffee table. He reached down with it into the hole dug next to him and set it to rest, his mother's ashes.

He lay a moment not wanting to let go, and he lay another moment after he had. Slowly he got up then and stepped back to his three children.

"Unto God's gracious mercy and protection," the minister said, "we commit you, Elmira. The Lord bless you and keep you. The Lord make His face to shine upon you, and be gracious unto you. The Lord lift up His countenance upon you, and give you peace, both now and evermore. Amen."

"Amen," Carl said.

"Amen," Mike said. He held Matt's and Janice's hands and held himself inside.

"Amen," Janice said. She buckled a moment and had to stick a finger beneath her glasses and clear her blasted tears. It was for her grandmother and for the young girl part of herself.

"Amen," Matt said. Everyone was saying it and so —so did he. He smiled.

It softly, softly began to rain.

26

"Bbbbmmmmwwwww." Matt said.

He was motorboating about his father's big bed. Carl sat on the window seat at the end of the room watching him. The crisscross of the laundry line wove behind him, white lacing against sunset sky.

"Come here, Matt," Carl said. "Sit down."

Matt motored over and sat on the window seat beside his father.

"I know we've told you before," Carl said, "but I want to make sure you understand. Your grandmother's dead. We're alone now."

"Yes," Matt said.

"You do understand?"

"Yes," Matt said.

"I don't think you remember when your mother died, do you?"

"No."

Matt watched his father closely. He wanted to say the right thing.

"She'd been sick," Carl said, "and she knew she was going to die. We lived with that almost as long as we knew about you. But when she died—it was still rough. A bear, Matt. This is going to be like that and worse. We're going to have to hang together. You understand? Your grandmom was the ramrod. She held together. She wouldn't give a rip for us if we didn't do it now."

"Where is grandmom?"

"Don't know, Matt. Like to say heaven, but I never thought much . . . believed much of that. Wherever the best go, she's there."

Matt said then:

"Will she be back next week?"

He hadn't understood, and his father put his head into his hands; he broke down. Carl, himself a strong man, doesn't understand it all, either.

"No, Matt," he said.

What Matt did understand was his father's grief, and he wanted to help. "She wake up soon."

"She's dead, she's dead, *she's dead.*"

He pounded the litany at his dumb son and it didn't help. The repetition, the trying to get it across left him only emptier.

Matt can only think of one thing to do: he puts his arms about his father.

"Be okay, Dad," he said, not understanding. "Be okay, Dad."

It was dark behind them now; the dusk was gone, the clothesline was gone.

27

The next morning a butter knife reached down into the toaster after a piece of toast. Mike pried at it with the knife and jimmied it and couldn't get it. The knife bent. He concentrated . . . he almost had it . . . he did have it . . . here it came. The knife snapped. Back went the toast. Now half the knife was down there as well.

Mike was not pleased: he banged the toaster on the kitchen table and then picked it up and shook it, half-ready to throw it against the wall.

"Senile toaster!"

"What's the problem?" Janice said, coming in.

"This thing doesn't work. Nothing around this place works."

"It works," said Janice. "You're such a spazola."

"Oh, yeah?"

"Yeah." She took it out of his big hands, set it down, and reached a slender finger down like a hook. Pop, there was toast.

Her skillful ease pleased Mike even less than the broken knife. "You are good for something," he said, grudgingly. "But what do I have to do—call you every time I want some?"

"I can fix it," she said, casually.

"Sure thing, toaster queen."

"I can."

"Just give me my bread. What's left of it."

"Boy, are you a *buttnik*."

"One more word," he said, "and I'll slice you into that senile machine."

Their rising voices had carried down the hall.

"*Hey*," Carl said coming in. "Some of us were trying to sleep."

"Mike couldn't even get—"

"Fold it, Janice. I don't want to know what it was about."

"Can I have my bread now?"

"You even burned it, didn't you?"

"Fork it over, Janice." They were starting again.

"Shut up, both of you," their father said. "And sit down."

"Want coffee, Dad?" Janice asked.

"No, and I don't want any buttering up. I want you to sit down."

Matt appeared, then, under his father's arm. He wanted to be part.

"Well, now that we're all here," said Carl, "maybe we ought to talk."

They all sat down, including Matt. Mike tried to butter his black toast fruitlessly. His scratching was the only sound for a minute.

"Without your grandmother here," Carl said, then, "we're all going to have to pitch in. I don't know how we're going to manage it."

Mike stopped working on his toast. He and Janice

looked at it and then at each other. Stupid, silly, small squabble. Mike pushed the toast aside.

Janice said, "I can cook and clean, Dad. I always helped Grandmom."

"...Okay."

"I can drive, Dad," Mike said. "Do errands. Pick up stuff."

"Okay." He was buoyed by their willingness, their enthusiasm. "...I'll farm out some of my long hauls, cut the schedule back. Gonna cost us some bucks. I'll have to get a second loan on things. Get ready for some penny-pinching."

They sat another minute thinking about the hole in their midst, what else they could do. Matt bobbed up from the table then:

"I clean toilets. I clean toilets at Washywish."

"...Matt, you've got to go back," Carl said. "Especially now."

"No, I clean toilets."

"Matt. We're gonna be lucky if we sneak by at all. Damn lucky."

"I run away," Matt said. "I run away again."

"What are you talking about?"

"He ran away," said Mike.

"He *ran* away? How'd he do that? How far'd he get?"

"Actually, he got in a truck and tried to drive it away and knocked over a sign."

"He got it started? He got it moving? How come we haven't gotten the bill?"

"I okay. I clean toilets." Then Matt said, absolutely disgusted, "The truck not have sixteen gears."

"You are something." Carl looked at his son: some

worry, some awe. The kid had done *something;* be it bad or good he wasn't sure.

Mike said, "The special school said they were ready to take him, Dad."

Janice said, "Mike could drive him and pick him up."

The two started sounding off again, one idea on top of another, this time on the same side for once. They ran down at last in the face of their father's not answering until there was quiet again. In his silence, Carl carried all the past failures and he carried his mother's wish.

"Okay, Pintsize," he said finally and uncertainly. "You're on."

28

The special section of the Wachataw school was in the old brick junior high. Carl drove Matt there the first time for his interview and some testing and a physical exam. Matt liked them all. In the interview, he got to tell what he liked most to do, basketball and running and construction paper and lassos—he had just discovered lassos. And his family, but unlike his family, the interviewer hadn't heard any of it before. He thought Matt's enthusiasm was terrific. In the tests he got to identify objects (good), match shapes (bad), and draw (best). His father said when he showed him his drawing it looked like the end of the world on a bad day. He didn't tell his father it was really just a lot of lines: he had pretended the pencil was an airplane and he had zoomed around the paper sky (zoom zoom). In the physical examination he got to stand on a scale and pull the metal ruler that came out of the top. They hit his knee with an eraser and his head with a fork and put a tire around his arm that pumped up tight. He even got to pee in a bottle.

In a couple of weeks, they determined that he did

all right, so Matt went to his first day of school. Mike dropped him off in the morning and told him to be out in front ready and waiting at four on the nose.

"No shally-shilly," Matt said.

"That's right. Four o'clock. You be ready."

"Fine," Matt said, and he danced into the old brick building.

Inside there were voices and feet and shouts and laughter coming from the classrooms, and Matt's dance wound down. He got first day jitters suddenly. He slowed up so much that he barely reached his first teacher, who was standing, waiting, outside her classroom door.

Her name was Heck and she was a wonderful black tyrant. She had been through riots and she'd been to the White House. She had been an artist who had fallen into teaching despite herself, and it had gradually consumed her life; it had become her cause for the past fifteen years. She shook Matt's hand and she showed him the art room. It was an unusual room: it had once been a locker room and had a concrete floor and high, wired windows and a row of basins and marble shower stalls. She worked around these obstacles. On her own time, with her own help, she had blown out one far wall to let in some light. It was a huge greenhouse window now. She could watch the light play on the children as they worked, as if she were drawing it, as if she might have time to. After her regular classes she worked with those who couldn't get into the school, those over twenty-one, the multiply handicapped, those with police records. She was a shrink in a sense, as well as a teacher, and she dispensed with typical behavior. She did the unexpected.

Some of her students loved to hug. To outsiders the groping affection was lovable, endearing, a little pathetic, but safe. Wilma Heck wouldn't have it: it was just a way out, a way to stay infantile. She peeled their limbs from around her, and she blasted them verbally. She demanded they take responsibility. Her seeming cruelty, the knowing chip she carried, always kept her near dismissal. She leveled with everybody and had a consistent ability to shock the bureaucracies surrounding her work. Do—gooders were aghast at her day-to-day reality. Only her results saved her.

Each year she put together a show of the work of the students and those who came after school. A surprising amount of the art sold. The artists got half the sales price. The other half almost supported the school's supply needs.

She asked Matt what he wanted to do, and he said he wanted to paste and to draw. There were many magazines he could take inspiration from, and tubes and tubes of paint, and lengths of shoelace wound into balls. The paint tubes were silver and, if used, rolled up from the bottom like toothpaste. Crumpled, open, they seemed run over and to have begging mouths. As for the laces, the balls looked big enough to lace up a whole basketball team. He started to work.

Just before the end of the class Mrs. Heck set up a videotape camera and playback machine. When it was ready, she stood in front of the camera. The students crowded around her in an uproar, seeking attention.

"Shut up, shut up," she said, and then looked directly at the camera. "This is an art class, and each student will illustrate a piece of his or her work to show you what we do here, and what they can do. For some of these artists who can't count, the number 'two' is of no use. Why should they then be force-fed it, if it doesn't stick? Why should it mean anything to them? They may not have great retention. They may have little yesterday and less tomorrow." She held up a painting: it was a pen-and-ink drawing of bicycles racing. There were wheels, spokes spinning, and backs bent. The wheels together made a fine tornado. It was a remarkable piece of work. "This can be their eternity. Art. A kind of immortality. Structure is so important, but it doesn't have to be the same structure for everyone. There are different ways of seeing and doing. And what it looks like isn't the same for everyone, shouldn't be." Then she said, "Who wants to be first?"

There were shouts and jumps: "I do. I do. I do."

"All right. Carole Ann. You first."

Carole Ann appeared in front of the camera and on the playing-back television screen. She was a Downs, short and dumpy, and her tongue stuck out because her oral cavity was so small. Words were slippery for her, like a soft owl-like cartoon character. It belied her considerable quickness.

"These are the pyramids," Carole Ann said, "I can put shapes together better than anyone. Tanana, the fat banana, thinks he's hot, but I know things better than he does. Here's my drawing."

She ran right into camera with it.

Bruce, sitting too close to the television, reeled from the oncoming pyramid. Then, laughing at his own vaudevillian take, he took a bow. He liked to take bows.

Wayne Tanana appeared on the screen then, and

Bruce blew a raspberry and laughed again. Tanana was big and wide, full of flesh, and he always rocked and almost always cackled. His cackle could combine with Bruce's laugh. They would sit together and practice the combination driving everyone beyond distraction. Wayne talked very fast, almost under his breath, and he loved insults. He said:

"Hee hee, blow Carole Ann's doors off. Can you dig it?"

Bruce covered his ears.

"I see Bruce," Tanana said. "I eat him up for breakfast, I puke him up for lunch, I shit him on toast for dinner."

"Wayne," Trina Cunningham, Wilma Heck's assistant, said, warningly.

Bruce stuck out his tongue at the screen, touched it, his ears still covered.

"You want to hear what else?" said Wayne.

"Your work, Mr. Tanana," Wilma Heck said, "show us your work."

"All right!" He made the words into a large long exclamation, and he held up what he had. It wasn't a painting, it was a sculpture made from pieces of soap. He showed it to the camera and belched.

Others belched, too; they loved to belch. They made an orchestra.

"Wayne," Ms. Cunningham warned again.

"Whoops, sorry. Hee hee," Tanana said and rocked from side to side. "See what I did, camera. Many bars of soap."

"He never washes. *Ooooh*," said Carole Ann.

"I wash you, can you *dig it?*" Tanana said. "I want to see what I look like."

He rushed over to the TV screen to see.

"Where am I?" he said then, crestfallen.

Bruce uncovered his ears but he hung close to the set.

"Now, who's next?" asked Wilma Heck. "Roger?"

Roger was a tall, lean, quiet boy, and he sat drawing a portrait at a desk from a magazine; he was careful and accurate and moved at his own pace to his own music.

"What are you going to show us, Roger?" asked Trina.

"No," said Roger.

"Come on, Roger. You do good work," said Wilma Heck.

"No."

His no's weren't rude, just definite. He kept on working.

"So we don't get to see Roger."

Bruce applauded.

"Bruce, you want to be next?"

Bruce hid his head.

"Only you didn't do any work, so we can't use you."

Bruce applauded.

"How about you, Tom?" suggested Trina. She inched Tom in front of the camera. "What did you paint, Tom?"

"I paint," said Tom.

"Let me see. Hold it up." Tom did. "That looks like a landscape."

"I paint a landscape," said Tom.

"What else is in the painting?"

"I paint a landscape," said Tom.

"But there are trees, and isn't that a rock, and a lot of leaves?"

"I paint trees, and a rock, and a lot of leaves," said Tom.

He was a good painter and he had echolalia; he repeated back virtually everything that was said to him.

"Thank you, Tom," said Wilma Heck.

"Thank you," said Tom.

"Now our new student, Matthew Gallitzin," Wilma said.

Matt was in the corner with his work, unsure of this ebullient group. He was also unsure of what he had done.

Trina Cunningham went and retrieved him and choo-chooed him through the other crowding bodies toward the camera. "Go ahead, Matt. Don't be shy. Don't let these wuhahas get to you."

Trina was in her early thirties. Her hair was short and red and she looked modern, without artifice. She wore pants, a tube top, and a blouse over it. She had come here to work after her marriage had broken up. Working with Wilma and the students exhausted her, but she found herself. For the first time she let go of what she had thought she was supposed to be, and became what she wanted to be.

The work brought some of the artists a long way; it had brought her as far. She could now dish out "Shut up's" as well as Wilma, the harsh cover for a limitless patience, a quiet zealotry.

Matt looked at the camera investigatively. He was silent, his paper at his side.

"Up with that masterpiece," Trina said.

For another second Matt stood still, and then he flashed his work: it was a red truck patched from construction paper and carrying a big, big ball behind it.

"What is it, Matt?" asked Trina.

"My dad drives a truck," said Matt, "and this is the biggest basketball in the world."

"That is silly," said Carole Ann. "No basketball's so big."

"What do you know about basketball, Carole Ann?"

"Everything," said Carole Ann.

Matt looked at his drawing, wondering.

Bruce looked at Matt's drawing on the television screen, wondering. He scrutinized the supposed truck and the supposed basketball and then he turned his thumbs very elaborately down.

Trina Cunningham said, "Maybe you should be a Special Olympian."

"I beat him," Wayne Tanana said, crowding toward the camera's range again. "Beat his buns."

"Olympics. . . ?" said Matt.

"See, Matt," said Jim, appearing. "Like me. I won." He spoke slowly and stood proudly and eased a medal from his trouser pocket and showed it off. It was worn bare of gold, silver, or bronze and dangled from a worn and wadded ribbon.

"Yeah, I bust his buns, too," Tanana said, grabbing the medal.

"Hey," said Jim.

They both roared off-screen.

"Wayne!" said Trina.

"Okay. Hee hee," Wayne said. And besides Waddles had sat on him, and he made even Tanana seem thin. Tanana gave it back.

Thumbs down went Bruce; he loved the gesture.

"Olympics?" said Matt, still thinking about it, still in front of the camera.

Dirty Raoul had had enough and stepped in front of him; he obliterated Matt's image.

"My turn," said Dirty Raoul.

And he held up a drawing of a snake's head in front of himself. Its huge tongue flicked, and then its body unfolded and unfolded and unfolded and unfolded, piece after piece of paper Scotch-taped together. The tapestry of snake obliterated Dirty Raoul.

Bruce hid his head.

He was still hiding it from the snake later when Doug Ransom told Dirty Raoul, "Put that snake away and get on the floor. Time for sit-ups."

The boys were now in the phys. ed. room. It wasn't a gym—it had been the other locker room and it had exercise equipment and showers off one side. The members of the class hit the floor at Ransom's command. They lay around a long bench and dangled their feet over it. Ransom led Matt to a bare spot.

"All right, Gallitzin, just because it's your first day. No slouching. Hit it."

Matt got down and watched the others and then began imitating.

"Squeeze those stomachs," said Ransom. "Bruce, put your hands behind your head. Not over your eyes."

Ransom circled them as they worked. He was a short, dark, powerful, balding man. He wore shorts and had a running guard's thighs. He could make them hop to; he was an unconventional slavedriver with a sense of fun.

"Come on, Waddles," he said. "No quitting. Get those hughmongus thighs into action." He did kind of waddle even lying down. "Thatta way, Gallitzin. Way to go. Show these veterans." Tanana giggled, and Ransom poked him. "Can you dig it, Tanana?"

Tanana loved it, and up—up they went, and then down again at wildly differing paces. One, Sauros, who had the sharpest nose, did them very, very fast. He gave all and a half.

They did more exercises and more exercises; and then, afterwards, Ransom took them outside. Matt was already tired; he was ready to quit; he'd had enough. Whatever Ransom had in mind he wasn't going to do. Ransom laid down some witches' hats on a blacktop playground.

"This is going to be your track. All you have to do is run around it. Got it. Get it. *Go*."

Matt wasn't sure what he meant, and then he realized he was going to get to run.

"Okay, you athletes," Ransom called. "Do your laps. Move it out."

They started to run, and Ransom watched them, whistle on a lariat around his neck, Adidas on his feet. They looked violently different from one another —size and shape, missize and misshape—yet they shared the creosote furrows under their eyes. They were a collection; he loved them.

"Come on, Sauros," he yelled, "you pug-a-lug. The rate you're going, your sister Dinah will catch you."

He rode them. He clapped his hands goading them on, as encouragement.

"Go, go," he yelled. "*Go,* you athletes."

And Matt heard him as he ran. He was Mr. Awkward, Mr. Flat, and Duck Foot. He was being passed, he was virtually last, but he smiled. He heard the word "athletes"; he heard the wind. He was *running*. He soared.

29

Sherrie said to Mike, "You kept me waiting an hour."

"I had to test the leg. Just a couple of extra laps and a Jacuzzi." Mike's hair was uncombed; he'd rushed from the showers. He was late and speeding, daring stop lights. Sherrie looked better than ever.

"That's exactly what you said yesterday. Ankle this, laps that."

"Our first meet's next week. I've gotta be ready. This year I'm not going to lose. I gotta win."

"Jocks are so boring," said Sherrie.

Mike screeched the Pinto station wagon to a halt in front of the old junior high. Matt was not standing there; he was not in sight.

"It's 4:20," Mike said. "Where is he? He's supposed to be here."

"You're late for me, and who cares? You're late for him, and it's a big wow."

"You can take care of yourself," he said. "Boy, can you take care of yourself."

"Compliments will get you nowhere." She was going to have none of that.

"Look, tomorrow let's take an—*outdoor*—lab. We'll study the pines and the pine needles. All afternoon."

"That'll be hot." Her sarcasm turned "hot" to dry ice.

He kept trying: "Must study nature."

"I use the library to study. And, anyway, you'll be late."

"This time I'll be on time."

"Sure thing."

"I will. I promise. Now where is he?"

"You will. You're sure. You promise." The sentences weren't questions. With each, she now upped the temperature toward kindling. He thought he was in control but she could stick him; she could sensualize him to kingdom come. Her silver jacket winked.

"Just one thing," she said, sliding across the front seat toward him. "Not one more word about running." Her rustling jacket rubbed him. "*Ever.* Deal?"

"Not one," he gasped.

"Okay, Mich*ael*," she whispered.

Her eyes were slightly hooded coming up to him and an odd shade, a dirty porcelain. They were her clencher, they were her melancholy: she seemed so near tears as her foil went all the way through him. And there were her opening lips for his.

And Matt knocked on the window. The lips and eyes retreated.

"*Now* he shows up," said Mike, and then he reached across and opened the back door for his brother.

Matt jumped in. "Guess what we did? Guess what? Guess."

"Learned to fly."

"No," said Matt. "That would be fun, though. Can you do that?"

"No, chumbo."

"We ran. Ran. Ran. Vrrrr-mmm. Rrrr-mmm."

"Him, too," Sherrie said in disgust.

Mike turned to the back seat, away from Sherrie, "What do you mean you ran?"

"Laps," said Matt. "Like you."

"Yeah, I bet. How many?"

"One," said Matt, but he wasn't sure. "One-half?"

"Yeah, right, Roger Bannister. Look, I run three miles a day, plus sprints, and by next week, it's going to be seven, and then ten. That's running, Matt."

"But—" began Matt.

Sherrie said, "Take me home."

"Why?"

"You put him up to this."

"You can't put Matt up to anything."

"I've had it. O.D.ed."

"But Sherrie, why? What is it?"

"Drop. Me. Off." Sherrie said. "Now."

"Sit-ups, too," said Matt. "That was before running."

"Shut up, Matt." Mike said.

Matt was very proud: "I finished last."

"I said shut up, Matt."

"But—"

Matt looked back and forth from one to the other of the stony faces in the front seat, waiting for release so he could go on and tell more.

"Vrrrmmm, vrrrmmm," he said, not very loud, as he waited.

30

Her hands were puckering and Janice was going crazy. Load number four didn't want to fit in the machine. It was the sheets, and the end of the last blasted one stuck out like a great limp tail. There was no way she was going to do a fifth load. How could there be so much laundry? She studied her puckers. The nurses in books girls were supposed to read always fell in love with doctors with clean, soft hands from many washings. Pucker doctors. The books made her throw up. She refused to read them and didn't want such hands. She wanted her grandmother's hands, great, gnarled gauntlets.

What she wanted didn't get the sheet in or the laundry done. Again she picked up the end and this time she just jammed it in and slammed the door. She held it closed and held her breath. When she dared let go, it stayed shut. She pushed in the knob and it burst into humm, water pumped in, it worked. No sweat. She moved to the next machine and got out the hot dry. Anybody can fold a shirt, her grandmother had said, one, two, three quickly done. Oh yeah. Janice couldn't match her grandmother's work.

There always seemed to be the lop sides, the loose ends. She wasn't going to let it get to her today. The way they went, they went, and she began to carry the tipsy stack up the stairs; the load was just high enough to hamper her vision.

She was halfway up when the washer started to go ka-blunk. It was actually moving up and down, a bucking bronco. Back down she went with the teetering pile. The washer didn't stop; it hopped and groaned. Setting down the folded wash, she put her hands on top, as if that might calm it. The ka-blunk changed to a kaa-lunn*ggg*. In alarm she reached out to the dial. Unsure, she went ahead and spun it, skidding through Rinse-Spin-Dry-Wash, and back again. The machine shifted cycles wildly and then, with a whush, stopped. She spun the dial again, and now nothing happened. The quiet was worse than the kaa-lunngggs. She opened the door and looked at the twisty sheets. She gave the nearest a pull: it wouldn't come. She jerked it: it wouldn't come. She was stymied and frustrated and a little scared. The heat in the cellar made her perspire and a drop slid across one of her lenses and smeared when she tried to get it off. The loss of vision did it—she heaved at the sheets, and fell backwards when they suddenly gave way. She got up and kicked the machine. The machine took the punishment, it didn't do anything at all, and her sneakered foot began to hurt. *She* hopped.

"You senile machine," she yelled. "You lousy, dumb, doggy, frabby, scroty, rotten, *doggy, dumb—*" She ran out of her own expletives and began repeating herself and then lost her voice and almost fell again. Away from the tripping sheet, she leaned her elbows on the huge, dry pile. She looked at it and then she threw it around the room. She threw it and then she dug out the rest of the sheets and threw them. They were heavy and hurt to lift. Wearing out, she plopped to the floor in a clump of them. "I will never, never, never, never do laundry again," she said.

Her father said, "What goes on here?" She hadn't heard him calling or coming down the steps, and it had been impossible for him not to hear her.

She didn't look up.

"What's the matter?"

Janice said, "I don't know if I want to do this."

"Do what?"

"Women are underpaid, you know," she said, and it began to come. "Built-in baby sitter, housemaid, cook, and don't you dare look at the lamb chops."

"Is that the smell upstairs?"

"Don't you dare look at the washing machine, either. It was the winner by a T.K.O."

"It's only one day," said Carl.

"I know!" That was exactly what she meant.

Her father came through the laundered battlefield and knelt beside her. "Hang in there."

"I thought I could maintain, Dad, pretty good," she said, and now it spilled, the whole telephone book. "But I can't reach the top kitchen cabinets, and Zach's such a caca brain, and I thought he wasn't a boofer, such a fribbly, scroty spider, and Matt pees in his pajamas, and I'm sick of Sherrie on the telephone. Gaga, that's all she does. She's so stupid and Mike thinks she's this fabulous tuna. She's an airhead, Dad, a real airhead." She was almost enjoying her pain now. "Earth to Sherrie, Earth to Sherrie, and superstar comes home and his neck looks like it's been attacked by a million golf balls and—"

Her father was four or five blocks back, just trying to follow.

"Ease up on the hammer."

"It's true, all true, and there's more."

"I'll bet. But who's Zack and what the hell's a 'boofer'?"

"You know."

"I don't know."

She made a sound.

"What?"

"You know a—fartknocker."

"Run that by me again."

"Fart. Knocker," she said, laying it in.

"Janice," he said, warningly.

"Well, he is, sort of, and I thought he was different and I should of known better and—"

"I won't even ask about caca brain and golf balls. But where do you pick these up? Who are you hanging around with?"

"Oh, Dad."

"Oh, Dad, *what?*"

"Everybody says them, and worse. You want to hear the worse?"

"I better not hear one word of the worse."

"Well, I'm not going to do the laundry any more. *Sherrie* can do it."

"Look, about Sherrie. Seventeen-year-olds like Zack are usually not interested in—." He struggled for the appropriate word—*"deep* women, you know. That comes along eventually, hopefully, and Matt does wet his pants now and then. It's gonna happen, and it's no big deal. Keep trying."

"Dad. But, Dad." And then she said, "They get all the attention. Mike's this stud. King of everything he does. He breaks his ankle and he's a bigger star somehow. And Matt's dumb."

Carl said, "He's retarded."

"I know," she said, knowing she had crossed a forbidden line without wanting to. "But that's what I mean. He gets all this special attention. They both do, and I'm trying out for yell leader and nobody cares, nobody knows, nobody'll be there, and I'll never win anyway. You see—and I'm only—*me*."

The last word was it, really it, and it took a moment before it came, and it hurt; and the hurt kept exploding inside her.

"Look, Four Eyes," he said, but she couldn't hear his gentle mocking. He reached down out of necessity into the well beneath his taciturnity. "After you have a child and it turns out to be retarded, you don't think you'll ever give a rip again. You don't want to try again. You're scared. But we did, your mother did. She was sick, but she wanted another . . . and you came . . . she was dying . . . and she felt saved."

The words from the well reached across the laundry, and she held up a sheet to hide her weeping.

"And I'll try and make the whatcha-ma-call-it tryouts," he said.

31

"But what about *me*?" Mike protested.

"What about you?"

"I already pick up the cleaning. I do the grocery shopping. I take the garbage to the dump. I get Matt, who's never where he's supposed to be, and this is this spring of my senior year."

Carl said, "Look, Mike, I appreciate your limo service. But Janice is getting a little buried."

"*She* is! Want me to go on with what I have to do, and this is my last track season. I've got to win the league, and I've got a chance at the state, if I'm in shape in time. My leg's *barely* recovered."

The telephone rang and he flew from the dinner table out of the room—some injured leg. "That's for me."

His father was left with the emptied room.

"Janice. Phone. It's Zachary," Mike called upstairs from the hall, mocking the name.

He came back into the dining room and flopped down. He picked up his last chop, looked it over, flopped it back onto the plate. Sherrie was supposed to call and she hadn't; what was going on?

"Senior year," he said, "and I'm supposed to be having fun. It's like the last chance I'll ever have, and all I get is burdens and responsibilities, and Janice—just doesn't know how easy she's got it. And Matt—Jesus, easy breezy." He glanced up from his plate at his father. "Don't look at me like that."

"Listen, Big Senior, we need your help."

"I'm overbooked. I'm already a one-man energy crisis." Then he said, "No human being could eat these chops." And he was gone a second time.

Carl sat and looked at the plates, four where there should have been six, and he would have liked eight. The sconces on the wall barely lit the room, and he sat alone. He finally got up and carried all the plates out to the kitchen and stuck them in the sink. He wandered around them. He couldn't remember when he had last washed dishes; check that; yes, he could—when Mike had been in a high chair, he and Mary Ann had done them together. It had been a high spot and he had sung songs to his son, who warbled and squeaked back and flounced his arms, like a spastic conductor. Carl had a big untrained baritone, and it went well with running water and babies.

He got out a beer now and turned on the hot water and found the cleaning liquid. He started to sing now as he washed. His voice wouldn't go where he wanted it to go, but it didn't matter. He had another beer. When the dishes were done, he scrubbed the counters, swept the floor, and sponged the refrigerator. He just worked now, he didn't sing. He had another beer and began to walk through the house. In each room he stopped, feeling it. You live in a house thirty years, and there's a lot in the rooms. The house had aged without his noticing. Barry Manilow and linty nerfs and sweat socks present, but the molding was also peeling. The rooms had begun to gather must, siphon light. He kept thinking it was last year it had been painted, and he had been thinking that for ten years.

He went through the hall closet. Coats stuffed its foreground, but behind and underfoot were the croquet balls and machine guns and card tables and plastic putting greens and a carved wooden sword in a cardboard scabbard. He rummaged in the rueful light, dodging the stored debris, stalactites and stalagmites, and stumbled on a dump truck. He bent down and studied it. There had once been a whole set, miniature Peterbilts, and he had struggled on a Christmas Eve to get them together before dawn. And here was one left, a burly dumpster, a tough toy. Its wheels whined across the palm of his hand in need of oil, and he had another beer.

He sat on the window seat a while, drinking, and then he found himself looking inside. There were no pictures of Mary Ann in the room, no mementoes. This was where he kept what he could of her. He could look at her in a bathing suit, smell a scarf, hear snatches of her voice in her scribbled letters. They offered up their drying sadness; there was a decade of distance now. He looked so seldom: there were things he had begun to forget, the way her hip bones showed in the bathing suit, and when was that taken? But he knew most: he had saved and stowed them; the cache was his formal mourning. After she died he kept discovering other notes, in books, between shirts, a few words sometimes left, jotted nonsense, and the slash of her initials, M.A. The words and the sudden wanting her—to feel, to fuck, to share—they better measured the loss. They cut right through.

He carried several more cans of beer outdoors to his Peterbilt. Capsizing the hood forward, he began to noodle with the engine in the dark. He knew most of the parts by shape, but he brought a work lamp out from the garage so he could really see. The engine showed the four hundred thousand miles and the care. The idle wasn't quite right, and he was worried about the gear box. "Just isn't working," he said, pulling his head out. "Isn't going to work."

He opened his throat and chugged another beer; his Adam's apple rode the wave. Finished, he crushed the can absently in one hand. He put it and the rest but one up in the cab seat, and leaned his head back down into the engine.

"Dad, you okay?"

Carl's head snapped up. Matt was at the edge of the garage under the basketball hoop in his pajamas.

"I—fine." He had to clear his throat between the words, the beer's effect.

"Can I watch?" asked Matt.

"You should be in bed."

"Always sleep. Not always get to watch."

"Nothing to watch."

"We ran in school today," said Matt.

"I know. I know," his father said. "You told us."

Matt came across to him, but he couldn't see into the engine; it was too high. And, instead, he climbed into the cab and sat beside the pack of beer.

Carl said, "I love diesels, you know that, Matt. This baby most of all. But its days are numbered. Truly numbered."

He looked up at his son: Matt was playing with the gear shift, the mirrors, the fan, quietly pretending, sort of listening. "Vroom vroom," he said, turning the wheel, content.

"You're the only one, Pintsize. We're falling apart. Broken eggs. And you're happy." Carl shook his head and kept working; and he kept talking. Wife dies. Mother dies. Family falls apart. Uneatable chops. Filthy toilets. Oldest son's at damned stage where he won't listen. You listen, but I never know what you hear. What do you hear? Best audience, probably. Your sister—her mother's in that flash behind those four eyes. She's going to eat hombres up. The language she uses. I don't even understand what she's talking about half the time. Where does she come up with that stuff? Booker, blooker—*boofer*. What is *that*? Wants to be a cheerleader or some damn thing. Doesn't need it. Smart as a whip. She'll be going to one of those expensive, snotty colleges and end up a nuclear physicist, and she wants to be a cheerleader. And your brother—he bitches. One of the finest natural athletes, sets school records, and some—airhead—has him spinning so he can't see straight. He should be spinning them. Maybe he is. Certainly acts it around here, the character. I probably ought to pound some sense into him. Your grandmother—she would eat him up. Make him eat those uneatable chops. Hasn't made his bed in months, or cleaned up his room. She could whip him into shape. Wasn't Elmira something? She could—sing. Did you ever listen to her voice? She could climb a mountain, build a snowman. I remember—oh, hell, the old man was alive then. They were out there together and rolling in the snow, my own mother and father, that bastard who had me scared straight out of my pants, and I see the two of them, both must have been fifty years old, throwing snow at each other. Big C got him." He stopped and then he said, "Elmira—she could fold a shirt. She could . . . What I ought to do is pack a shirt and hit the pike. Highball it. There's a lady out there I'd like to talk to. Give up all those long hauls. Hell, my days are numbered."

And then he said, "When you were born, and when Mary Ann was strong, and when there were going to be many boys, we were going to build some trucking firm. Gallitzin and—Sons."

His voice had dropped, so soft; and the man who didn't talk much finally ran down. He began to worry about how much he had said. He looked up into the cab and his son was stretched out, asleep.

Carl went to the open door. "Did you hear me? Did you hear any of my nonsense?"

Matt's eyes opened an instant: "Dad!"

And then they closed, and his father looked at him again. He wiped the grease on his hands off over the callouses on his butt that bound in his million-mile bounced bones, and he picked his sleeping son up, and carried him into the house.

32

Mike felt good before the race. Limbering up, he felt completely mended. The ankle gave him no pain; he hadn't a sense of it at all. That was what he needed. He got down into the blocks just to feel his confidence and kicked his legs one final time loose. He got up again and shook his arms out. He loved the mile, the competition was a cinch. Easy breezy.

Halfway through the race his stride was good and loose and long. The runners whipped by the wooden stands into the third lap and he took time to glance at Sherrie. In the third place, he rambled on, holding back, showing off. The next time by the stands everyone accelerated. This was the gun lap. Mike stayed on the shoulder of the runner in second place. When that man made his move in the backstretch Mike hung with him. Their feet kissed the cinder. The man grabbed first place, the old leader quickly dropping back. Mike passed him, too, but lost a step, then another. He knew, then, he had been wrong about the cinch and the easy breezy. It wasn't the ankle or the other runner, it was everything else. He was just a shade enough out of shape.

He tried to go faster, find his sprint. He forgot Sherrie, he forgot his ankle, his strategy, his showing off. They were down to the final quarter of the final lap, and he was still two steps back. He had to do it now and he dug into himself beyond the sore and the hurt, and the passing gear was there. Arms aloft, he snatched the race at the tape.

For fifteen seconds he felt really good again, and then he began to die. His hypnotized mind gave itself back to his wheezing body. His lungs burned and bent him. He was *dogged*.

Matt reached him then. He was clapping still, all excited, and he picked up the dragging tape and ran it around Mike. "Mike win. Beat Chatcan. Beat Doctor Roger. Win win. Run Gallitzin run. I run, too."

And klunkily around he went with the tape.

"Teach me, teach me," he said.

"Are you kidding?" gasped Mike, when he could again talk. "I'm barely alive, and I'm not a teacher and never going to be."

"Teach me, teach me."

"Well, if I were, first you got to—" Matt had him half-tied up now, and Sherrie was there.

"You were fantastic, Michael," she said.

"Matt, cut it out," Michael said, and to Sherrie: "Walk with me up to the locker room."

"I've got my car."

"Leave it. We'll come back."

"But it's full and waiting," she said.

Across the field the Firebird was waiting and full, an assortment of girls, and Sarnowski in front and Connolly leaning out the back window.

"Come on, let's go," Connolly yelled. "Time to rampage."

"Teach me, teach me," said Matt. He still ran around Mike and Sherrie, especially Mike, and Janice had come from the stands and picked up their trail.

"You heard the man," Sherrie said.

"You better go ahead," Mike said. "I'll meet you."

"Well, I *guess* I can wait while you shower."

"Well," Mike said, reluctantly. "I don't know if that'll work. I've got to take the fry home. I'll meet you."

"You always have to take somebody somewhere," said Sherrie, "and it seems never to be me."

"You could come with us."

"My car's better, faster, and *it* has a muffler."

Connolly yelled again, *"Time to rampage."*

"I going to learn," Matt said. "Run run."

"Shut up, Matt, will ya." Mike fended off his brother's motorings.

Sherrie said then, "It's now or never, Michael."

"Come on, Sherrie."

"Come on, Sherrie, what, Michael?"

"Don't do this."

"Do what, Michael?"

She looked dead at him without flinching, and then she turned and walked to the Firebird and got in. She looked so good walking away. He stood absolutely torn, his victory stripped away, his brother and sister lead weights.

She didn't pull away immediately. She let him look at the Firebird full of his friends, full of her. And she watched him as the car idled, waiting. A part of her hoped he would come at the last minute; a part of her wasn't sure what it wanted. The uncertainty built like anger against the desire to give in. He waited too long, and her bravado won. She floored it, waving from the window. She knew then, even as she forced a smile, she hadn't wanted to go; she knew then she felt terrible. She knew she was never going to show it, he was never going to know, and he was going to pay for it.

33

Hundreds of mobiles tinkled and turned. They were suspended from the ceiling, a balletic blizzard. The class sat at benches beneath them making more. Matt poked holes in the soft, pigment-shade clay. He had made several already, and they waited around him, like numbers on a clock. His were men, gumbo-shape men, and he pounded and planished each with great concentration. This was like how his grandmother cut cookies, except Ms. Heck said he couldn't eat the clay. Of course, he couldn't before it was baked, but then why not? It was different, she said, a 'killer,' not an oven. Matt tried to chime like the mobiles did. That was hopeless. After giving that up, he babbled a song of sound until he thought of commentating.

"He in fourth, he in third, he in second," he began then. "Around final turn, Gallitzin head and head. It Bannister. It Gallitzin. It two Gallitzins. Mike and Matt, Mike and Matt, Mike and Matt. Gallitzins win! New record!"

Trina Cunningham, moving from student to student, checking their progress, heard his call. She listened to the outcome as she watched him work and the mobiles play.

"What are you doing, Matt?" she asked.

"Making holy man," said Matt.

"No," Trina said. "What are you talking to yourself about?"

"My brother won. He run. I gonna, too."

"Where you 'gonna'?"

"I don't know. But I run."

"But you get to run in gym."

"Fine. But." He strained for correction, for the difference. "But run really. Really really run."

Trina said, "I remember. You are interested in track. Aren't you?"

Matt looked up from poking: he nodded, a big nod.

"You really like to run?"

Matt nodded, a bigger, bigger nod.

"Then you should be a Special Olympian. Do you know what that is? Do you remember what we said?"

He shook his head, a big shake.

"Well, Mr. Ransom and I will just have to show you."

"Now any one of you can be a Special Olympian," Ransom said, that day after school. He stood on the blacktop playground, a whistle and a stopwatch around his neck, a horde gathered around him. "All you have to do is try your best. We'll try you at different events and see what you like. There are track and field events, there are—"

"I've heard this all. Mr. Ransom, you talk too much," Bruce said. "Let's get with it."

"Bruce," said Ransom.

"What?"

"Stick it where the sun don't shine."

"You hear that. He told me to—" Bruce was outraged, and then he said, "What do that mean?"

"Hee hee," laughed Tanana.

Carole Ann said, "Bruce, you are a dumphead."

"What she call me?" Bruce looked around in further outrage and astonishment, the incredulous innocent. His sense of theater was as broad as Mae West's.

"Dumphead. All right." Tanana stretched it again to the moon and squeezed then "Can you dig it?" into virtually one and a half syllables.

"I'm Number One," Bruce said, in his own defense.

"I'm Number One," Tom said.

"Shut up," Bruce said to Tom.

"Shut up" and "Shut you up," said Tom and Wayne Tanana simultaneously.

Doug Ransom said, "The next one who opens his mouth gets sat on by Waddles and me and maybe even Tanana. We don't want talk. We want workouts. We want athletes. Not everybody, Bruce, has competed before. They may want to know how it works."

"I'll tell them," said Bruce.

"Okay, you tell them how many times we're going to practice every week."

"Two."

"Wrong. Three."

"That's what I said," said Bruce.

"What days?"

"A-a-a-a, Tuesdays, Mondays, and—Tuesdays." He didn't know the other days of the week.

"Wrong. Monday, Wednesday, and Friday."

"That's dumb."

"Why's it dumb?"

"I said so."

"I think we'll ignore you for a while, Bruce."

"*Yes*," the others said.

Bruce flipped his thumbs down, and was ignored.

"I want to tell what I did last year," Jim said. "I ran fifty yards and I got to dress like Charlie Chaplin. I wore a coat and a cane at the dance the night before. I wore a coat and a cane like this." He did a dignified duckwalk, a legato Chaplin. "I'm going to be an actor."

Bruce flipped his thumbs down, and was ignored.

"I was on the floor hockey team," said Waddles. He stuttered when he talked, so often he didn't talk. He just acted: slowly stood up, slowly sat down, sat on someone, smiled, groaned, watched. He talked now because he was proud. "I stopped the ring and stopped the ring. Every time they shot the ring at me I stopped it."

"Wait a minute, Wad," Ransom said, "What about when—"

"Almost s-s-s-st-t-t-o-op-p-p-ped it," Waddles said.

"He was good," said Carole Ann. "Big and slow and he lay there and that one dumphead put it over him. No fair."

They talked in turn about how they had competed, what they remembered, what they could articulate, or about what they were going to do. It was a highlight of their lives. Tanana had a story about his baseball throw and Higgenbottom had a story about how he wanted to try the long jump and Shirley Wazniak had a story about the wheelchair race, except she really couldn't talk. Her head listed violently to one side and she jangled her arms and her vowels.

Sauros, on the other hand, didn't like to talk, he tried hard instead, while Dirty Raoul thought action was louder and better than words. Then there was shy Jacey Bendel, whom Matt had not seen before. She had long loose russet hair and a strikingly handsome face. The bones sat high and the skin fitted and the upper lip had bow enough to curve a wide smile. Her eyes were even handsomer, a luminous gray like dark ice; they were also deeply crossed.

Roger was alone in that he didn't want to do anything. He came out to say no and to draw portraits. The practice time offered him another hour and a quarter for his slow, meticulous work.

With Trina's help, Ransom laid out mats for the long jump and set up a foam high jump pit. They set all the athletes running again around the witches' hats to loosen up. After that, they began to test them at each event.

Matt tried them all. He threw terribly, he high jumped very badly, and he ran. That was what he was best at—he was only bad. His throws slipped out of his hand or went straight into the ground. He couldn't get his legs to lift off on the jumps. He knew they were supposed to—Trina told him, and Ransom ordered him to, but he didn't know how they were supposed to. The bar went down, it always went down. It didn't matter to him, even if he and the others had a long, long, long way to go. This was what he had always wanted.

34

Buh wop buh wop buh wop buh wop

Janice had emptied the closets and the bureaus and made a pile on the bed. She sat in the middle of the clothes and the boxes and the shoes, wearing a large set of cultured pearls, a necklace and earrings. They were all of her grandmother's things. She had to pack them and she was stalled.

Buh wop buh wop buh wop buh wop

The job had waited for her and now it had taken days. She seemed to only get a little done each time. She kept discovering things that she didn't know about her grandmother and now could never know, and they tired her out so quickly. She was just ready to try to start again, and now Matt had to wreck the toilets.

Buh wop buh wop buh wop buh wop

The noise stopped then, and a minute later Matt marched in, carrying his bucket and his plunger.

"Where are you going?" Janice asked.

"I clean toilet."

"You know it's backed up. It'll just overflow *again*. Do the rest of the other ones."

Matt went right on through.

She looked at the ceiling for help. "Grandmom, how did you stand it? We offer him your room so he can be alone and he doesn't want to be alone. He wants to stay with Mike, who doesn't want him, and now I'll have to clean up the entire bathroom floor."

The sound came again, like a finger popping out of a cheek.

Buh wop buh wop buh wop buh wop

Matt played the floor with his plumber's helper. He didn't stop; he was on his way. It almost belched, yet it was almost music. He raised it then and plunged it into the toilet and kept on going. He plunged and plunged and *galumpphh*. It started to move, it started to clear, and *whush,* it went. Matt lifted out the helper and started playing on the floor once again.

Buh wop buh wop buh wop buh wop

Janice had gotten up and come to the doorway to yell at him. She watched his prowess in disbelief and came over and tried flushing the toilet herself. She bent down to watch as she did. Down it went cleanly, and her glasses—raised on top of her head—fell into the middle of the flush.

Buh wop buh wop buh wop buh wop

"Help. My glasses, my glasses."

Matt stopped: "Glasses?"

"My glasses went right down."

"See. Works."

"Oh, no."

She went to put her hand in after it, chickened out. The lid was ajar and laid catty-corner and she jerked up the ball. Everything stopped.

"It's your fault," she said, furious. "You did it and

without them I'm a total spazola. Instant quadriplegic."

"I still like you," said Matt.

"My glasses!"

"Okay."

Without rolling up his sleeves he reached into the water and down the hole. He fished.

"Are they there?"

He fished deeper.

"You'll probably come out with a baby crocodile. Are—they—there?"

He fished and fished and up his arm started to come, slowly, slowly, and there they were, intact. He handed them, dripping, to her. She put them on as they were, and then, unable to speak, she kissed him, and ran from the room.

Matt touched his face with his hand where she had, and then looked at his hand. There was nothing there but he could feel the place she had touched on his face still. The ball let go, the flush completed itself. The water hopped, which he liked; he rubbed the porcelain shiny, which he liked. Job well done. He did a few more practice plunges on the floor for good measure.

Buh wop buh wop buh wop buh wop

Janice sat back on the bed with her grandmother's things and heard the sounds. She took off the necklace and the earrings and was going to put them into one of Elmira's stocky-heeled shoes. Before she could, she broke down. She didn't understand it, and she couldn't stop it. She held the pearls and wept.

Buh wop buh wop buh wop buh wop

35

Sherrie could drive Mike crazy. He was cool and an athlete, and in shape at last. He shouldn't worry about these things. Why did he, then? Her bellybutton—thinking about it, the tight way it twisted practically into an outy, and he could feel it in his stomach. His gums ached when he was tired, wanting her. And sometimes she'd give a little, a feel here, a bare breast there, and then she'd take it back. The next time he wouldn't be able to get it. There was no satisfaction. It was like a game of peekaboo, of chicken.

Call her a cunt and be done with it, he would think, and the next time she'd be all there when he needed her. She was more like cat than cunt, playful, willful, but her own when she wanted to be. She could twist words, twist *silences*. He never knew when she would phone, and when she did whether it would be gay or disastrous or almost without words. He tried to keep his hands off her to keep control, to show her, but couldn't, and she seemed to know. She always seemed to know, and she would punish him or not punish him at her momentary whim.

There never was a consistency, he never knew how she was going to act. She kept herself as behind the darkest of glasses. He wanted to break her, he wanted to touch her. He had always wanted games, but before he had always been able to win.

The time he got away from her was when he ran. He forgot himself a little then, and thought about other things and about nothing at all. For its moment, he could listen to his breaths and to his feet and not his mind. Running healed, and he had won race after race. He had never run better or needed it more. Now the league championship was only a day and a half away. He was favored, he was ready, he was going to win, and last night they had changed, and tonight might be even better.

They had committed a crime last night, but that had been the beginning. At the end she had been so different it had thrown him entirely again. They had broken into her father's office. He had no idea why she wanted to. For one thing, she could get anything from her father, certainly a key. She made it a dare, though, a secret mission, and he found a window to jimmy. It was high enough so he had to lift her in. She wore the softest sweater, and he could feel heat pouring through.

Once inside she knew where everything was, the lights, the three patient rooms, the clean and dirty needles, the drugs, the medical books with the best pictures. She toured him through all the rooms; she couldn't keep still. She had come a lot as a child, never any more.

In one closet were her father's white gowns, and nurses' dresses besides. The dresses surprised Sherrie. They hadn't been there when she had, and she had never met her father's new nurse-assistant, Iris. She insisted on trying one on. She was in the bathroom long enough to make Mike edgy. He worried about where they were and what they were doing, and he turned off all the lights she had turned on. So the bathroom backlit her when she finally came out. She had never worn anything so tight or so translucent.

Sherrie was small; Iris must have been smaller. Sherrie could wear clothes that grabbed, Iris maybe, too. Inching the uniform on, Sherrie thought about how Iris must look and how it must peel off. She set out, right then, to seduce Mike. She had had to take off her sweater to get the dress on, and she didn't stop there. She tossed her underclothes after it.

"Where are you? I can't see you," she said, coming out. "Michael, Michael, come out wherever you are."

The backlight played behind her head and between her legs. He could see what was missing and what was there.

"I'm here."

"What happened to the lights?"

"We're not supposed to be in here, you know."

"That's why we are here."

"What?"

"To do what we're not supposed to."

There was starch in the uniform and it sizzled as she found him out. What she wore always seemed to sound.

"Sherrie," he said.

"What do you want?" she said. "Tell me what you want."

"I don't know."

"Mich—ael."

"What?"

"Tell me."

He took the uniform into his hands and bent her over the examination table. They hit the paper laid there, another crackling. He touched her where he hadn't and her crotch was wet. She held onto him and let herself go and he lay on top of her. Her legs parted and hit the stirrups. They spun and sounded like horseshoes landing, and her chest shuddered. It kept shuddering, and he didn't know what it was. He wanted to think it her peculiar passion until he couldn't deny, even in the dark, that she was crying. He closed her legs and held her then, and his wanting gentled into a deeper, just as mysterious, land.

She took it while she needed it and held onto him. She had cracked and was going to hate herself for it. She had never cracked so. For once she had lost control, and she had wanted to get him, to make him, and to shaft him, and he almost had her.

She got dressed in her own clothes, and wadded Iris's uniform into her pocketbook, and they climbed out as they had climbed in. She couldn't yet think or set herself. She didn't know what to do, what it meant. She held to him tight on the way home. By morning she would know that was a first gift she had to turn into a final carrot.

Mike came up from practice early and saw her Firebird near the back of school. He hadn't realized she would be there, and he went in search for her before showering.

"No practice today?" Connolly said, coming up to him.

"Came up early for a Jacuzzi."

"You just better win tomorrow, hot shot."

"I will."

They walked to the library together and Mike looked in for Sherrie and didn't see her. He walked on down the hall and past the library's second door, and gave it a glance. He just saw her then. The door was the entrance to the back stacks and had only a small window, and she was just visible wrapped into Sarnowski's Belmondo lips.

He stopped, he froze, he died, and she opened her eyes then. She looked at him as if he were stone. She looked at him without wavering, without flinching, and then, deliberately, she went back to Sarnowski and opened her mouth to his. She had done and did now what she thought she had to. She had no choice, she had to protect herself, didn't she? She couldn't back off, she had to go through with it now, didn't she?

He turned and walked away.

36

Matt had never swum before and he jumped into the pool and down he went, down and down. He didn't know what to do and he couldn't breathe. Water came in when he tried. They got him out, spluttering. He would try practically anything, but he had no intention of going in the pool again. Water fascinated him, the way it jiggled and could splatter. The pool was interesting, too. Sounds echoed, and the muggy air almost made the skin wet before you ever got in and went down and down.

The others had all swum before and weren't bothered. They yelled and splashed and their avid, blubbery flutter kicks made huge poolunks and kerplunks that sounded a little like a plumber's helper. That made him kind of want to try again. But Jacey Bendel intimidated him. Her strokes were rough, but she had a surprisingly fluid kick and her long hair when wet sleeked back as smoothly against her head as if she had been a porpoise. So good, she turned his recklessness shy.

Trina worked with the swimmers, cutting through their hacking around and their laughter at how funny someone else looked. She made them keep trying. She walked beside them as they attempted lengths, her own maillot suit spotting from their splash. She bent with them as they dived, instructing them how not to belly flop. They belly flopped anyway, but she didn't give up. She encouraged, wheedled, haggled, complimented, cajoled them into one more and then one more. She had them imitate her, and she never stopped talking to them. The talk became a stream and not specific words. It taught but was even more a lulling of possible fear, a safety net. She offered them consistent attention, something many of them had never had.

Trina believed in swimming. She knew the soothing of it herself, and she believed there was a connection between swimming and coordination and between swimming and the power of speech. The first wasn't that hard to figure—swimming used all the limbs and had a simple rhythm that had to be retained and repeated. The mind and limbs made a sustained connection or down you went. She didn't understand why it helped speech. She had read a study about it, and she had seen it. The speech center in the brain was somehow exercised simultaneously with the limbs. Children learned similarly: they saw an object and recognized it, and then they started reaching for it. They wanted to touch, to grab, to mouth. The mouth and hand were as connected as the eye and hand. Only after then did they begin to warble words and not just sounds.

Trina was aware of Matt not swimming, and she had a solution. She saved ten minutes at the end for him and tried to talk him into the pool. He shook his head, a big no. This pleased her: he remembered what had happened last time. She couldn't break his determination down, so with five minutes left she picked him up and threw him in. The difference was she threw him in the shallow end. He went down, but there wasn't depth to go down and down. He could touch. He stood up in surprise. "See," she said, "there's a bottom and nothing to worry about." He wasn't convinced. What was a *bottom?* He had gone down and down. He started to walk toward the side of the pool to get out. She cupped a hand and skimmed the water, splashing him. He kept coming, and she chopped a bigger splash. He yelled in protest, but she kept it up. He changed direction, and she moved around him, blocking him, splashing him. The splashes weren't hard, and his panic gave way. He would show *her*. He tried to splash back. It wasn't much of a splash, but it was exactly what she wanted. He had made a motion approximating a stroke. He closed his eyes and splashed and splashed at her until he was laughing.

She worked with him then beyond the minute left, got his belly down, his face in (sort of), his arms and legs thrashing. He didn't go very far, but now he didn't want to come out. A pickling prune, he had found fun and the first tenuous fragments of skill. With the safety of her words and her strokes (and the shallow end) he learned there was something other than going down and down.

37

Yell leaders weren't cheerleaders, of course. Cheerleaders were so blatant. Janice always felt as if they were all letters on their chest and panties in cartwheel. Tits and ass. Sure she envied them, but she wasn't a *Cindi,* a *DeeDee,* a *Sukie.* She really wished she played the sousaphone. That's what a girl should do. She wasn't put off by its horsecollary size and weight, and she borrowed one of the school's two so she could try it. It *was* a monster, but it was almost as much fun to wrestle with and blow as she had imagined it might be. Control and modulation were another story. The mouthpiece was as big as a shot glass and made her lips ache. She could make squawks and groans, little else. She couldn't carry any tune or any base line. She kept borrowing it for an hour in the afternoons, anyway: she would show them next year. This year she was going to be a yell leader.

She had to learn to move her arms and to cup her hands around her mouth and shout simple things. She practiced in the cellar so only the laundry would see her foolishness. The yell leaders worked behind the cheerleaders but in front of the drill team who in turn sat in front of the band. Zachary played the saxophone. There was more than one reason to yell and to take up the sousaphone.

The tryouts were held in the gym and she wore short shorts and knee socks and saddle shoes. She looked tight and terrific, but she was sure all the others looked good and she looked terrible. She was a bundle of excited nerves. She kept sneaking her glasses on one last time. There was so much to see between the terror. The judges were Mrs. Marin, her gym teacher, and Miss Delvecchio, the guidance counselor, and also the two co-captains of the high school cheerleaders. As much as Janice could muster mockery for the megaphone queens, these were still gods, and she wanted to see them, how they acted, what they did. The glasses cleared the fuzzies, the mire of myopia, but she really didn't get to see. Having them on made her even more self-conscious, capable of only the most oblique glances. Her glasses off again, she couldn't see the others who were trying out, her friends and enemies. On again, she couldn't really see them, either. She was too wadded into waiting on her own turn to gauge good or bad or wish luck.

The sight she missed was fifteen girls giving all their hearts. For this instant this was the biggest and only thing in their lives. There was sweat and work to it, energy and brightness, and yet a moving melancholy. They couldn't all make it. Their yells caromed into the corners of the gym and came back, but each for her moment was alone.

Janice put her glasses on one final, ultimate, absolutely last time before her turn and saw her father coming in. She remembered what he had said, but she had been trying to forget it. She was sure he wouldn't make it and didn't want the disappointment. Trying to forget only made her remember more, but, now, there he was filling the doorway, holding Matt's hand, and it changed her. His presence, her brother's small wave. She took off her glasses, and she let go. She had hung on so tight, the adolescence in her. It didn't matter now suddenly. There was her best to do, and she did it, and there was math, and all the ups and downs, and Zachary, maybe, if he didn't turn out to be a total boofer, and there was herself, and next year there was the sousaphone. She had some time to fail because she was going to succeed.

38

He had managed to live somehow through the day and a half, and he was in the lead. Mike had forgotten about her totally, and he was in good shape. He wasn't going to be brought down by some girl, he was more mature than that, and he was cruising along. Life wasn't easy breezy, but he had it in hand after all. He was running full out, sure of himself, only forty yards to go. He had it, and he relaxed and started to raise his arms toward victory.

It was then he heard footsteps, heard the oncoming exhalations. Someone was catching him. He looked over his shoulder, always a mistake. It took time and it splayed concentration; you couldn't go as fast forward looking back. And there was also no one there, there was no second place now. In just strides his lead had disappeared.

His attempt to accelerate crumbled his stride. You couldn't do it on a dime. From a start you could burst, but in full stride it took time and yards. He hadn't them.

They went through the tape together and Mike had won. He knew he deserved to win, anyway, so close, and he could have beaten the other guy any day, and—he had been robbed. His luck, his ankle, the fluke of it, the weather, Sherrie—oh, Sherrie; he tried every rationalization and every one failed, left him lower. He was still on the track, still trying to get some air. His lungs burned so. He bent down and down and felt sick. He had lost, there was no escaping it. He had let himself down, there was no escaping it.

"Pinto," Mike seemed to say, much later.

"What Pinto?"

"It was here."

"I told you he wasn't of age."

"He had I.D.," the bouncer said.

"They all have I.D. Now which one is it again, kid?" the bartender said.

The dragging figure between them spoke, kind of spoke. "Pinniac."

"Could you translate that? You know he's heavy. He's a big kid."

"Stachu wagu," said Mike.

"Station wagon. There's one. Come on."

They grappled Mike toward it.

"It's a Pontiac. *That's* what he said."

"That it," said Mike.

They jammed him in.

"Now go to sleep before you drive anyplace," the bartender said. "And easy on my parking lot."

"I loss. I loss," said Mike.

"We got the drift, kid, about six hours back."

Mike slid over onto his side, and they closed the door.

"It's enough to make you a prohibitionist," the

bartender said as they left. "And go into basket weaving."

"I loss," Mike said. "Tee. I loss tee. There's tee on loss. I know there is." His eyes closed, he passed out.

An hour later it began to rain. The metallic fire of the first drops snapped his eyes open. He had no memory of anything. His mind was empty. He lay a minute watching the water wriggle on the windshield. He closed his eyes again to go back to sleep when he started to remember. The race came back, and right behind he remembered Matt: he had forgotten to pick him up.

He got the station wagon into gear and out of the empty parking lot. He sped to the special school, slaloming through the rain. Fear had him wide awake and falsely sober. Stopping, he missed the curb at the school, jumped it, and fell getting out. His brother wasn't there. He pleaded to the rain: "He didn't wait for me. Oh, Jesus, let him be all right."

He got back in and lurched off. His increasing worry drove him even faster. He put the hammer down and misjudged a curve. He waited too long to turn, then turned too much. The station wagon wouldn't come back and swam off the gutted shoulder. He braked and knew that was wrong. The car glided on it right toward a pine. The needles waved and elongated in the headlights, like a nightmare. On it came. He dropped the brake, downshifted, popped the clutch, and the car kicked, as if jump-starting. It didn't stop the slide, just slowed it down. It seemed to take almost forever before it hit.

Mike got out and went up into the headlights and tried to separate car from tree. His feet kept slipping as he pushed. He heaved, and before he knew it he was on the ground. The station wagon hadn't moved.

"Got to get home," he said, but he couldn't get up. He decided to lie still just for a minute and watch the rain in the lights. He couldn't do that, either. The world wouldn't stay still. He turned over and just made it to the tree before he threw up.

He was still after he had nothing left inside. "I'm wrecked," he said to himself. "I'm totally wrecked." And he let his head rest against the bed of needles.

After a while, when he could, he stood and started for home. He came back to turn off the lights and get the keys and started again. It was a cold, wet slippery several miles. He walked and then he began to run. At first he would stop when exhaustion made him, and then he wouldn't let it. The race of his life, he ran all the rest of the way.

Only when Mike arrived, he saw there were the lumps and folds on the other bed and his brother buried beneath. Matt was home, safe, asleep. Mike went over and sat on the edge of the bed. He watched the lumps and folds lift and fall, his brother's wheezy breaths. It wasn't enough. He peeled back the covers and shook him awake.

"Mike!"

"You all right? You really all right?" Mike asked. "You got home. How'd you get home?"

"I swim."

"What?"

"I swim."

"That can't be," said Mike. "You really okay, chumbo?"

"I fine."

"I didn't mean to forget you. It's just I got problems. Women, and all I cared about was winning and I lost, and I got totally wrecked."

He was still a little wrecked and he lit a cigarette, not very well. Matt watched.

"It's all over," Mike said then, "I'm going to smoke now and learn how to blow smoke rings and smoke until I die of nicotine fits. What the hell does it matter? My life is over. We'll both go back to Washywish together and grow old and get moss-covered and they'll put us under together."

"No Washywish," Matt said.

"I didn't mean to forget you."

"No Washywish."

"No Washywish."

"Fine," said Matt.

"You go back to sleep."

"I swim," said Matt, and he lay back down. He went back to sleep, as if he had never completely waked up.

"You'll probably never want to ride with me again," his brother said and pulled the sheets back into their original chaos.

When he got up, his father was in the doorway.

"You all right?"

"I'm all right."

"Tie one on?"

"No. A little, maybe. Yeah."

"Did it help?"

"I don't know."

"Next time, call. Let me know. Okay?"

Mike nodded.

"We were lucky someone saw him. We were lucky I wasn't on a haul."

Mike couldn't even nod.

His father said, "Sometimes I want to poke you, Mike. But you're almost a man. You don't need to poke a man."

His father turned his back on him then and left him. Mike hadn't let only himself down. There was no escaping it.

39

Wap wap wap went the shade shooting all the way up and rolling into itself after Matt released it. What was making such a noise? Mike didn't want to know. He didn't want to wake—his head, the hour, the clear bright light—and his brother was shaking him. He tried to fend him off.

"Wap wap wap," said Matt.

Mike covered his head.

"I wake up. Wake up," Matt said. "I need ride. Special Olympics practice."

"What?"

"Late. Late."

"Go away."

"You take me."

Grumbling, reluctantly, Mike opened his eyes and sat up. He had gotten out of only half his clothes the night before, and he started trying to get his legs into the muddy trousers that had been dropped to the floor. "What am I, an on-call chauffeur service?"

"Late. Late."

"I need food."

Matt tried to help Mike get ready. He ran to the

closet and got sneakers and tried to put them on him, the wrong pair on the wrong feet.

"Matt, what are you doing?"

"Special Olympics."

"What are you *talking* about?" Mike got to his feet, one leg in, one wrong shoe on, and then the night before really struck. "Oh."

"Got to go," Matt said. "Got to go."

"Will it never end?" said Mike in lament.

The night before already had fallen away—almost. He kept complaining, but he kept dressing, picking up the reins of responsibility despite himself.

They had to borrow the car next door, and Matt didn't stop talking the whole way. As soon as they reached the brick junior high, he ran from the car. This was their first weekend practice, a mini-competition before the area games at York. Doug Ransom blew his whistle and a fifty-meter race began. Instantly, the four-hundred-meter competitors lined up around the new, now slightly scuffed, starting line. Matt just made it to the line in time.

"Way to go," Ransom yelled after the fifty-meter runners. "You're late, Gallitzin. Almost missed your four-hundred. *Behind* the line, Hunsucker."

He blew his whistle and off went the four-hundred-meter runners.

"Come on, Sauros. Come on, Waddles. Move it, Gallitzin."

Mike turned to go and stopped. He watched his brother a moment. Matt was game, he hung in, but he fell behind everyone but Waddles. His legs went almost in circles, rather than forward and back. It was a joke, except for the rapture on his face. Even Mike could see it. Losing, probably going to kill himself, but he was still having a great time.

Mike shook his head in disbelief. He watched the others, some equally bad. They were a small group but in such high spirits. Finally, he started the car. He had to go rescue the Pontiac, measure the damage, see if it would run, and then get back to pick Matt up.

After the four-hundred Ransom spoke to Matt: "Your hands should go like this, Matt." He pistoned his arms as an example.

Matt pistoned his.

"Real good. Now try it."

Matt ran pistoning, then soon forgetting.

"Hold it," Ransom said. "Get back here."

Matt came back.

"You got to keep it up. Pistons."

"Pistons," said Matt, and practiced. "Rrrmm rrrmm."

"That's it. Now the same thing with your legs—"

"Mr. Ransom, Mr. Ransom, my baseball went over the fence. Hee hee," interrupted Wayne Tanana.

"Okay, Banana, we'll get it. Now, go, Gallitzin. Let her rip."

Matt did, arms better briefly, feet the same, clump, clump. Ransom watched and got ready to call him back again.

"Mr. Ransom, Bruce hit me," said Higgenbottom.

"He hit me," said Tom. *"Too."* The additional word was his own, a victory as great as the hurt of Bruce's gleeful punch.

"Bruce," shouted Ransom. "Bruce the Moose."

And he was hit from behind and had to turn to choke Bruce out, and was instantly surrounded by four or five others wanting his immediate attention. He had to let Matt go.

The four-hundred was to be one of Matt's events. The athletes could compete in two, plus a relay. His second event was the high jump. Trina coached the high jumpers near the end of the practice: "Come fast, but not too fast, and jump high."

Matt concentrated when his turn came and trotted up and jumped, hitting the bar on his way up, knocking it off. He wasn't disappointed at his miss, even though he barely got off the ground. Such a short way up, it was a shock to anyone watching. But he loved the going up, no matter how small. Even more he loved the coming down, he loved the falling.

"You've got to jump sooner, Matt. Get up before the bar."

Trina lowered the already low bar and had him try again. He missed again. He always jumped the same way, despite her instructions.

"We'll get there, Matt," she said, and he got back in line as she turned to help the long jumpers. She, too, could only give him so much time.

He wasn't worried about it. He was already looking forward to his next jump, his next flight. The wait in line made him so anxious he jumped even sooner this time. Up he went, barely leaving the ground, and he almost missed the pit. The edges of it had extra bounce and he lay there perfectly satisfied, the bar on top of him. He looked up at the clear sky, still bouncing.

In the middle of the sky, replacing the sun, Mike appeared. All the way to the Pontiac and back he had been thinking about the few minutes of the practice he had seen. He was embarrassed by his brother's spasticity, yet captured by his excitement. The enthusiasm was infectious—it drew him in and gave to him in his morning after, and he could give back—it would be easy to give Matt some pointers, show him how, help him; and that would lessen the embarrassment, of course.

"You gone," Matt said.

"I came back."

"You too soon. I jump."

"You jump? You call that jumping?"

"I like," said Matt.

"No, no. Get up," said Mike. "This is how you should do it. You step off ten paces at an angle, stop, turn, plant your lead foot and then run and jump. See. Try it."

Matt listened and was ready to try. He walked off some steps and turned. He concentrated very hard, waiting for an opening to jump, and then he ran just as before, plowed through the reset bar on the way up just as before, landed as happily as before.

"Oh, my God. I give up."

Matt danced out of the pit and caught up to his brother, walking away.

"Good. Good?"

"That was terrible."

"I like."

"The worst."

"Oh," Matt said, then, "I get better." It was half a question, half a statement.

"But you don't listen."

"But I love to jump, to run." And he began to do the one and then the other right there. "Most of all of anything."

"You do?" Mike said. "You—*really do*."

Matt made the biggest of big nods and Mike's half question became a full statement, a realization.

After the practice was over Mike drove Matt to the high school field. The grass was summery now, full-blown, and they had a bigger, better foam landing pit. Matt tried it out as if it were a trampoline. Mike finally had to pull him off to get his attention. Matt was extra excited.

When Mike did calm him down and get him practicing, what he thought would be easy wasn't so at all. For a full hour he didn't lose his patience. Then it was too much. His frustration blew his temper:

"No. No. *No. No!* I tell you exactly what to do. I list step by step and you ignore it. You do the same thing every time. Ten times. Twenty times. Who knows how many. Who can count so high? You're going to kill yourself and I'm going crazy. It's hopeless."

"One more," said Matt.

"You like punishment?"

"One more."

"Forget it. It's all over. I tried. *I quit.*"

Matt asked. "Fosbury flop?"

"If you could do it."

And Mike sat down on the foam beside his brother.

"You're never going to get better," he said. "What are we going to do? What am I doing here?"

"Teach me, teach me," said Matt.

Mike realized Matt wasn't asking, he was answering. He loved his brother and he had always dismissed him. But Matt wouldn't let it lie. He didn't accede to it or accept it, and he always came off the wall. He could always reach into Mike, catch him.

He was so straightforward and so simple. The power of it baffled Mike and laid him open.

"Some teacher," he said. "Where did you ever hear of Fosbury flop?"

"I do."

"Sure you do."

"I—learn." It was both demand and plea.

The two sat there, the only two on the field, and then Mike got up and reset the bar at two feet four. He watched it shimmy until it was completely still, thinking, and then he grabbed Matt and paced back with him from the bar at an angle.

"One, two, three, four, count with me," he said. "Seven, eight, nine, ten."

"Seven, eight, ten," said Matt.

"And turn. Look at the bar."

"Turn."

They both did.

Mike said "And plant a lead foot. Plant your left in front. No, like this."

He showed him, he physically moved Matt's foot. Matt pulled it back, Mike planted it again.

Mike said, "Left foot lead."

"Lead left."

And they both did.

Mike said, "Dig in that foot."

"Dig."

And they both did.

Mike said, "And run."

"Run."

"Picking up steam."

"Steam."

And they both did. They ran stride for stride.

Mike said, "And just before the bar, plant the same foot, the left foot, and use it to spring."

"Same foot."

They stopped at the bar.

Mike said, "Kick the right high and it will pull you up and over."

"Kick."

Mike slapped his right leg as indication and Matt slapped his leg, and Mike kicked his high, and, from standing, cleared the low bar easily. And Matt tried it: his leg went up and over but he forgot to jump, and Mike said it too late. But the leg had gone up.

"All right," Mike said. "That's what we're going to do. We're going to break it down. One step at a time."

They stepped off again, one to ten, and turned again and dug in again and ran again, Mike holding onto Matt's hand. Mike planted his left foot, and planted Matt's foot, and Matt planted his own foot, and Mike slapped and scaled his right, and slapped Matt's right and scaled Matt's right, again and again. Matt slapped his own right and scaled his own right, and Mike jumped and over Mike went, and Matt jumped a little and over almost Matt went, and Mike talked, and he didn't stop talking and showing, encouraging, the words insignificant in themselves, and it was slow work, slow, slow work, and the differences were fractional, *fractional*. But the differences were there, and unlike the laces, this time he took the time and worked, and there was a question now as to who was more excited.

"All right," Mike said. "Good, good. Okay, okay. Keep going. Keep on. Plant and kick and leap and turn. All right. That's better. Keep going. That's it."

Matt planted and kicked and jumped and hit the bar. Then Matt planted and kicked and jumped and just tapped the bar, and then Matt planted and kicked and the bar jiggled and it didn't fall. So Mike set the bar two inches higher, each inch a giant magnitude, and Matt planted and kicked and knocked it down, and it was almost dark and the sky was orange and then dark gray, and Matt planted and kicked and Mike talked and coached and cheered, and Matt cleared.

"All right!"

40

Mike found it increasingly difficult to stay away from Matt's practices. He got a continual charge out of being near so much energy and so much improvement. That was part, but not the deepest part. He had also loosed something inside himself, a beneficence. It flooded from him easy breezy, and embarrassed him, yet it made him feel good.

Doug Ransom spoke to him one day as the competitors charged around the witches' hats. "Everybody needs a skill, and these athletes sometimes try harder than any others. They care about winning, but not so much about losing. They just like most to try." He yelled then, "Real good, Sauros," and turned to Mike: "You've been here several times lately."

"Oh, I just drop by to pick up Matt."

"Mmn-hmn," Ransom said. "Now you're cookin', Bendel!" And then he said, "The area meet is this Saturday in York. Why don't you come along?"

"I'm pretty busy."

Matt ran by, his legs going nearly straight forward and back.

"Way to go, Gallitzin. I saw smoke comin' from your shoes," called Ransom. And to Mike: "We can always use the help."

"Well, I don't know, I'm not sure I can."

"Shaping up, athletes. Real good," Ransom yelled, and back to Mike: "Whatever you say."

That Saturday they all got to wear clean white T-shirts and dark blue shorts. They had uniforms. Matt was still studying his when the gun went off to start the race. The gun didn't surprise him—Mr. Ransom had used one the past week to rehearse them and help them get used to it—the start did. At least they could have waited until he had finished inspecting his shirt.

His late start left him last, and angry. His enthusiasm stretched tight into effort and he made his way through the field. He reached third place and clung to it around a turn and put his eye on second. His determination grew. He inched up and made it by. The boy was his own size, but the one ahead was *big*. He was determined, and he ran harder. There was no way, though, he was going to catch him.

And Mike was there, beside him, yelling. He had not been able to stay away. He trotted behind the smattering of coaches and Red Cross volunteers, yelling, and Matt's determination just grew. He motored, he really motored.

There was always someone called a hugger to congratulate every runner at the finish in the Special Olympics. But Matt didn't stop, he didn't hear the cheers, he motored. Mike had to chase him, run him down. He was still reluctant to stop.

"That was the finish line. You've qualified for the state meet," Mike said. "You won—athlete."

It sank in then, and Matt's gritted determination gave way to pleasure.

41

Mike found it difficult to miss a practice after that. Ransom and Cunningham had their hands full, so he started to offer his help, not only to Matt. The athletes came to ask of him as well as of the coaches, a demonstration, a word or two. He soon had his own crowd surrounding him.

He worried about being mocked when he wasn't there—what would his friends say—but he never thought about it when he was there. The amount it bugged him dwindled; you can't worry and have so much fun at the same time. His athletic seasons were over, but the rest of him was just being born.

The measure of his insanity was the relay. The runners had concepts to learn as well as running to do. Concepts were tricky and difficult. They could lodge one minute or one day, vanish the next. The athletes had to learn about passing lanes, about timing their starts, and about the baton. The baton was an alien object. It didn't look like anything in particular; it had no easy, exact connotation. This plastic or metal thing of one color or another with a hole in it. It was easier to look through it or use it as a weapon than to understand it was to be passed from man to man. Working together was its purpose. Try and explain that, concretize that. They tossed it or hogged it or panicked at it and dropped it or didn't start soon enough or at all or slowed down or stopped before reaching the following man.

He ran it with them, he held the baton out, he received the baton, he held the arms of passer and passee, and brought them together. He did it again and again. The baton became part of their lives, as did his instructions:

"Hold it up. Hold it out. Pass it hand to hand. Start to run, Matt. Before he arrives. Keep running, Hunsucker. Now time your acceleration. Now come on, Dirty Raoul, same thing. Hold your hand back, but be going forward. Soon as you feel it, you go. Get ready, Sauros. Hold it up, hold it out, Raoul."

And the athletes practiced—Hunsucker to Raoul to Sauros to Gallitzin—and gradually the comedy and the frustration and the sadness became awkward, and awkward became workable and workable became almost fluid. The combine whipped in and out of the passing zones, delighted with themselves.

"Take your time until you get it right. Time yourself. Time that pass," Mike yelled. *"Now you're smokin'."*

42

Carl Gallitzin hadn't found staying near home easy. He had to hire men to make the long hauls, he made less money, he had to be at the office to check their progress, log their work, and he discovered all the paperwork he had always tried to ignore. He was accessible, but he felt like he was home even less now.

He loved the road, and now he lived in a paper world. Work was paper, dying was paper, living was paper, money was paper. He hated it, and he bitched to himself, and he worked as hard as he ever had. He converted part of the old porch into a second office. That was the worst—moving paper from one place to another, shuffling it. In addition to everything else, numbers and details and invoices, organization and delegation and bureaucracy, exhausted him. Paper was fatigue.

He regretted it with every self-serving fiber of his body and brain. The only thing was, he was sure it had been the right decision. He had made Janice's whatcha-ma-call-it tryouts, even if she lost. He had almost made Mike's championship race (the same day as Janice's tryout), even if he had lost. The losses were interesting.

Janice had staked her life on the outcome, and then it hadn't bothered her. She rose from the ashes instantly. His shirts were still tye-dying from erroneous measures of bleach, but Janice was changing. Her glasses, her looks, her room, her studying. She had lost weight (they all had) but put on shape. She looked bigger—figure that out. She was as sarcastic, as sharp, as angry as ever, but her test scores had leaped. She still insisted cleaning the Peterbilt cab was her job and then still usually didn't the few times it was home any more, but she also was ready to teach him bookkeeping. She would happen into the porch office and poke around, bothering him, and check his figures, correct them. She thought his methods were stupid and simplified them. He'd come back and find his work redone, and she was right. She was as quick as a computer. She talked on the phone to some boy with a funny name, and he appeared at the house, but she never went out on dates. She hadn't really started to have them, and she said she was now too old for them, and, in a way, she was right. It didn't stop other boys from calling and hanging around either, and there was a girl friend who was as big as Carl was. She had a boy's name and was practically a woman. She had that much size and carriage, and she had no idea she had it, how close she was, any of what it might mean. Janice seemed to know about her friend, and about herself, and about so many of those meanings now.

Mike had staked his life on the outcome of his race and ignored his brother and gone out and run the car into a tree. The tree had wiped out Detroit. The damage to the tree was a three-inch loss of bark; the car was five hundred and fifty plus next year's insurance jump. Maybe it was lucky in a way; the call about Matt not being picked up had made him remember Janice's tryout. Mike had forgotten about the car and the loss almost as quickly as Janice. He seemed to have hit bottom in one night, yet he hadn't changed, had he? All he talked about still was athletics, track and relays. Whatever happened to football and baseball, the American sports? He seemed to have given up girls, which was highly unlikely. He seemed happy, though, even exuberant. Carl wondered what was going on. He would just have to wait for the next explosion. "The star" Janice called him, sarcastically. He wished he could tell Mike how easy it would be to invert her sarcasm. He had brains, and all the scholarship offers. He moved too fast. If only the rest of him would catch up with the gifts he had already gotten. How do you tell a kid and not make it sound like it always has before? Such a son.

And Matt, he hadn't thought much about Matt lately. He realized that wasn't insignificant. He had spent so much time thinking about only Matt when Matt had been young, and them displacing it. The retardation was always there, haunting you. Was it your fault; what could be done? And when there were no answers, he still occupied your daily existence. You always had to know where he was, keep him in that kind of sight and safety. Carl hadn't been able to do it with all the other things, which was one reason for Washaminy. Now he was home and it had no right to work and it hadn't been and yet now—they were still alive, they were existing, they were sneaking by. Even if the rest of the bathrooms looked like war, the toilets shone. Matt seemed happy too, even exuberant. Carl didn't know what to make of it. God, kids were mysterious.

Carl thought about these things as he polished his shitkickers, his driving boots, sitting on the window seat. He did them and did them again, practically a spit shine. The scuff of the brush became part of his musing and the sound of the front door didn't really register nor the first call of his name. It took four pounding feet on the stairs to break through his revery, and then his sons were in the room.

"Dad!" they both said.

"Now what is it?" He kept on polishing.

"They've asked me—" Mike began.

"Run and jump," said Matt. "Olympics."

"One at a time."

"This weekend, Dad, and they're going to be twenty-two hundred competitors from all over the state and Matt's qualified in the four-hundred and the high jump and the relay and they've asked me—"

"Run, jump, hold it up, hold it out," said Matt.

Carl had to look up. "What are you talking about?"

"The Special Olympics, Dad," Mike said.

"What the hell is that?"

"Dad, I've been trying to tell you. We've been talking about it for weeks."

"Is this what you've been going to in the afternoons?"

"Yeah, Dad, and they've asked me—"

"Wait a minute. How's this work?" Carl looked at Matt. "You qualified?"

"Run, jump, hold it up, hold it—"

"He sounds like you," Carl said to Mike.

"*Dad*," said Mike. Fathers were such a travail.

Carl said to Matt, "This is important to you. You really want to go to this..."

"Special Olympics," said Matt.

"How much is this going to cost me?"

"It's paid for, Dad. At least Matt's way is."

"*Matt's* way. What does that mean?"

"I've been trying to tell you. They've asked me to come along as an assistant coach, and—"

"How much will you have to pay?"

"Half. Seventy-five dollars. But it's a big thing, Dad. There'll be thousands of people and track and basketball and swimming and floor hockey. They've all qualified in area meets. One guy ran the mile in four-fifty!"

Mike lost his attempted low key. His enthusiasm took over despite himself. So much so that Matt started to talk, too.

"We all ran and I in group three and—"

"Some of the times are amazing," said Mike. "You ought to see it, Dad—"

"—and in group four," said Matt, "and Jacey's in group two and run and—"

"It's like..." said Mike. "I don't know what it's like. It's like nothing else."

Carl said, "This is really it, huh."

Such nods, and they both started talking again, gobble gobble gobble.

"What the hell," Carl said.

43

Janice packed Matt's things into a real suitcase. She took the clothes from his bureau and folded them. His uniform had YORK across the chest. She put it in with some socks. Mike lay on Matt's bed, watching her work, throwing a ball against the wall.

"Hey," he said, "those are my socks."

"I know," she said. "They shrank when I washed them."

"Everything shrinks when you wash it."

But she was gone, and Mike looked above his brother's bed and the open suitcase to the four posters on the wall, two of himself. He began wondering about that person there and himself, and then Janice was back in the room, carrying a windbreaker. She packed that, too.

Mike said, "Where was that?"

"I had it."

"You swiped it. You're as bad as he is."

"We're the same size," Janice said.

She tossed in a sunshade from Matt's hat collection and a Ben Hogan-like golf hat, and then sat on the suitcase.

199

"You're so good at that, you should do mine, too."

Snap, snap went the case.

"You know where you can get off," she said and jumped off and was out of the room again.

She ran into her own room. A suitcase was on the bed there, too. Hers. She sat on it, and *snap, snap*. The whole family was going to go.

44

Alma Rennseler Riley always saw his rig before she saw him, but not this time. She had about given up on ever seeing him again, and now he filled the window, getting out of a station wagon, not dressed for the road, accompanied by a young man, a girl-woman, and a short excited boy. They came in and he walked down the long counter to her and to his accustomed seat.

"Hello," he said.

"Coffee?" The lack of truck, the changes in him made her cautious.

"One one-hundred-mile brew," Carl said, and turned to the three sitting down around him. "What do you characters want?"

Two wanted to look at menus and the third, the short boy, spun on his seat and hummed.

"This is my family," Carl said. "Mike. Janice. And Matt. And this is Alma. Say hello to Alma."

They exchanged hellos, but Alma didn't know what else to say. She hadn't expected this. She didn't know why they were here, what it meant.

"So this is it," she said. "I've heard about you."

"I hope he didn't tell you the truth," Janice said.

"I know you look like your mother."

"I do?"

"You do," said Carl.

"I know Mike scored thirty-one points against Smithfield, twenty-eight against Marshall, twenty-six against Lantenengo. Do you want me to go on? I know you're an even better runner."

"Who is *she?*" asked Mike.

"She's your agent," said Janice.

"No, your father's your agent," Alma said. "He's only told me each statistic five or six thousand times. It was easier to learn them than take the chance of having to hear them another five or six thousand."

"The kid can play basketball."

"The kid can play basketball," she mocked.

Mike hadn't known his father was such a storehouse, he never seemed to listen or care about any of it, and Janice had never heard anybody mock her father, even so gently.

"What should we know about you?" she said to Alma.

"What does she mean?" Alma said. "Is she a wise guy?"

"She is definitely a wise guy."

"I've worked hard at it," Janice said, "And am proud of it."

"Just ignore her if you can," Mike said.

"I like her," Alma said, and Janice stuck out her tongue at her brother.

"Order. *Now,*" their father bellowed, more ebullience than threat, and they did.

Alma took the orders and reached Matt, still spinning. "You haven't even looked at the menu yet, and I don't know anything about you. What do you want?"

"I'll order for him," said Mike.

"I order," said Matt. "I have potato chips and pizza."

"You can't have that. You're in training."

"I like."

"You can't have it also because we don't have it," Alma said.

"Have a milkshake," Carl said.

"Yeah!"

"What kind do you want?"

"I have potato chips and pizza and milkshake."

Alma looked at Carl who looked back. "He'll have a vanilla—"

"Coffee," said Matt. "Coffee."

"One coffee milkshake. And give him a fork. He doesn't need it, but otherwise he's bound to take mine."

Alma said, "One shake, coffee, one fork, coming up."

She had other customers to keep her busy, and she glanced at the four of them when she could and got back to them as Matt sucked at the bottom of his glass with his straw. Emptiness didn't faze him.

Alma said then, "This is the one who was delivered in the rattletrappy dump truck, isn't he?"

"Yes," Carl said. "That's right."

She said, "You could have told me about him."

"He's retarded." The statement had just its own natural weight, no emphasis, no blurting, no hiding, no shame.

"Yes."

Carl said, "It's Matt who's brought us here. We're on our way to the Special Olympics in Lycoming. He qualified for the state games there."

She said, "You must be proud of him."

Carl had to clear his throat. "It is an honor."

"Lycoming's only ninety miles from Wachataw. How come you stopped here?"

"We had to stop."

"Toilets," explained Matt.

"Toilets," Carl agreed. "And some unfinished business."

"What unfinished business?"

"Alma . . ." he began, but the start of his statement also became its finish.

She seized upon his taciturnity. "Are you sending messages, Gallitzin?"

"And you better receive them," he said, gruffly.

"She turning red," Matt said then.

"Shut up, Matt," Carl said.

"I am not. No such thing, no way, I am not. I'm just glad to meet you all. Really am. There's no getting around it."

"You sure can talk."

"I can be quiet, too, guy," she said. "And this is on the house."

"We'll see you then on the way back," he said.

She watched them leave and Carl turned a moment and looked back at her, the fingers of the pines behind them, and then he corralled his excited, retarded son in a mild headlock. She knew then they all had a place now in Carl Gallitzin's life, the three that accompanied him, and she, too, with her hundred-mile brew.

45

Matt had been allowed to drive with his family, but he stayed in one of the college dormitories with the rest of the team. He was the first one there by only a minute. He had been in rooms like it yet *not* like it before. He started to lug his suitcase toward a bed when Wayne Tanana, who was going to be his roommate, boomed in. He went immediately to the window and looked down the five stories.

"I'm going to get Dirty Raoul's shoes. Drop them off. Hee hee. Can you dig it?"

"He blow your doors off," Matt said.

"Bust my buns," Tanana laughed.

Dirty Raoul appeared. "You got my shoes?"

Tanana cackled.

Raoul accepted that as a yes and closed in.

"No shoes," said Matt.

"Daggg," Tanana said, "somebody beat me to it."

"Better not be you."

"Who, me?" said Tanana, innocently. "You scare the mess out of me."

"Girls, then," said Dirty Raoul. "Where are the girls located?"

Tanana rocked: "Got to check them out, brother."

Mike poked his head in: "Forget girls, Dirty Raoul. I'm your chaperone, and it's time to shower and get you snazzed up for your photograph."

"My shoes first, then I get ready," said Raoul, and he dribbled his real basketball down the hall.

"Damn. No girls. Hee hee," said Tanana.

Raoul was the last one to be ready for the photographs. He was a slow dresser, not from lack of know-how or coordination, but narcissism. In addition, he discovered how the toilets flushed: you stepped on the handle and super *whush*. He had to try them all, and everybody else did, too.

They lined up at last for the photographer. Tom and Shirley held the banner. It shook a little in Shirley's wiry askew hand, but she held tight. Matt was in the first row because he was short; the three coaches stood in the back.

They posed and the first shot snapped caught them very serious, while in the second they laughed at themselves; it was all hijinks and grins. In the third, many were caught off guard, looking the wrong way, lapsed looks and closed eyes and bad grins. The fourth was almost right, and the fifth was it, as close as possible, serious and hijinks and great pride, and it captured, also, the fact of what they were.

The opening ceremonies were just like for a real Olympics, the athletes in procession area by area, old and young, male and female, blind and wheelchaired. They all came in their uniforms, marching as best they could, more than two thousand of them, waving and walking around the stadium track. They weren't normal, but they were kids, and many older as well—people, different, but not so very. They had feelings and pecking orders, battles and best friends.

The York team came and mixed up in them were those from Wachataw, Waddles and Dirty Raoul and Hunsucker and Higgenbottom and Jim and Tom and Bruce and Tanana and Jacey Bendel and Sauros and Matt, and the coaches. Others from York were in the stands, chaperoned, who hadn't qualified, but who had come to cheer, like Carole Ann.

An athlete ran the Olympic torch into the stadium and halfway down the track he passed to another, a girl who ran it back the wrong way until she was straightened out. She climbed the steps of the stadium then—over a hundred, without tiring—and with a little help leaned the small flame over the big tub. The big flame rose and the crowd cheered and the Downs girl with the little flame looked at it and grinned behind her glasses and her heavily braced teeth. The Special Olympics were declared open and a blind boy sang the "Star-Spangled Banner." He lost the words after "perilous flight." He stopped and hesitated and hung his head and then brought it up again and started again. The crowd joined in, everyone joined in, high voices and low voices, good voices and bad.

The Special Olympics Anthem was sung and then the special California anthem. "How far is far, how high is high, we'll never know until we try, until we try," and balloons were let go. There were thousands of them and they filled the sky. They rose into the dusk and became slowly, slowly small clusters of colored pinheads, and then there was just night.

At the dance that night Jim got to wear his coat and

cane, and Tanana sang and danced by himself, slowly turning to his own lyrics. Tom could repeat the lyrics of most of the songs nearly endlessly without mistake because the songs repeated themselves nearly endlessly. Shirley Wazniak tapped her one good foot. Higgenbottom wore half a tuxedo and was very dashing. He served punch and smelled the flower on his lapel until it wilted. Dirty Raoul behaved himself and was crowned king. He held onto his basketball throughout. Waddles went home early to practice his floor hockey moves. Bruce gave up trying to turn his thumbs down. Too many people were having too good a time, including him. He even danced with Trina. He loved movies and thought he was Fred and she was Ginger. He swept her with great low strides across the floor, a bowling Groucho, and, even if she wasn't Ginger, she came to believe he was Fred for one night. Matt didn't dance, but he watched Jacey Bendel dance. The only places she wasn't shy were the pool and at such a party, the only places he was. She could still beat him in a race. They had taken to competing against each other, and she was truly good. He got to watch her long hair, like a flag flapping, from behind. He was catching her, though. After each dance she came over to him and he got to watch her eyes. Some people said funny things about them but he loved to watch them. They could look at him in two different places at once. She was only an inch taller than he was, and during the last dance she stayed with him. He didn't know what to say, and she didn't either. They didn't speak, and he reached out for her hand.

Doug Ransom wasn't at the dance. He was a state coordinator of the games and all the coordinators and other high officials met over coffee for a brief planning meeting.

One, Robert Willoughby, was very concerned about the media handling of the games. He didn't want any exploitation of the fact that these people were a *little* different, and he certainly didn't want anybody to find out about the mad toilet flushing that had been going on earlier in several of the dorms. It would give out a false impression, put things in a bad light, distort the truth. They didn't really act like that. It was like last year's belching incident, *distortion, atypical,* and it reflected badly on all of them. The lid had to be kept tightly on these things.

Another, Simon J. Flowers, was worried about the security at the college. He had been asked personally about whether there were locks on the doors and, of course, there had to be. At the institution he headed, all the rooms had new, one-way locks, a terrific development. When reporters or whoever came to inspect or visit, he could always open them and show plainly how they weren't locked. The bars on windows were a more difficult reality. They didn't look good, and he hadn't yet figured out a way to do away with them with great fanfare while in fact keeping some equivalent.

Doctor Adrian Santuna was worried about a script that he had heard existed and didn't want to see (had anyone a copy?) about the Special Olympics. It apparently depicted doctors in a blatantly fallacious light. It had them talking wildly out of the dark ages, and one specialist in retardation saying something like he didn't understand a specific girl's unhappy mental state. Someone kept asking him to get more specific, who was doing it, what were actual examples, were they hiring actors or real people? He didn't have any answers exactly on hand, but it certainly was shocking and shouldn't be permitted.

Ronald Myerson had a beef with the Kennedy Foundation about permission to—and he was quickly quashed. Beverly Ziegenfuss wanted to know about her time as acting m.c., when was it to be and for how long, and how come Roger Etherington got longer, and who were these celebrities, anyway? Ron Masak, who was he? She had never heard of him. Where were the *names*? Who was in charge? That brought a debate and some heated words, and there were other debates about other important matters after it.

Ransom finally suggested they might consider getting to the actual business of the meeting and rehearse the logistics of the next day's events. By that time everyone was ready to leave. The coordinators alone stayed on, and the brief planning meeting went on far longer into the night than the dance.

At first light Mike had Matt on the track. They walked between lanes of fresh lime and bits of it blew like a fine flour. Workmen marked the lanes ahead of them, pinned up bunting, roped areas. Otherwise the two were alone.

Mike said, "After you come around the curve, remember, hug the inside, hug the inside. Never look back. Just keep running, you hear me?"

"I fine," said Matt.

"I won't be able to coach you in the high jump. I'll be working with some of the others. Ms. Cunningham will. But in the four-hundred I'll be there.

"Okay."

They walked.

"Just do your best," Mike said. "That's what matters. That's what's winning here."

Matt made the slightest nod and stepped carefully over the lanes so as not to touch them. They might be like cracks, and you could break somebody's mother's back. It made him watch his shoe, and at the edge of the grass he bent over. His shoes were untied. He worked on them, fruitlessly.

Mike bent down beside him, helped him out. "You are amazing. How do you do it?"

"Good grannie knot."

"Good grannie knot!" Mike had to clear away little clots of dirt, like handsome turds, that had been dug to sink water into the field, and sit to work on the monster of a knot. "After this is over, we're going to work on your grannie."

"Teach me, teach me."

"If we can teach you to high jump, maybe we can teach laces. Maybe," Mike said. "Now pull your socks up. Pull *my* socks up."

Matt carefully pulled the socks up until they were stretched smooth and reached nearly to his knees.

As Mike watched his brother he wondered, in fact, who had taught who.

Before nine the stadium was mostly full, with umbrellas and parachutes to make shade, and the field was crowded with competitors, and sponsors and huggers, all volunteers. Many wore white shorts and red shirts, striped or solid, bright and faded, a crispness to them like clothes fresh from the line. There were many of them, mostly girls, and from a long distance, they were a bright pageant against land and sky, and the smells of grass and Orange Crush filled the air.

The first race was for the littlest, the twenty-five-meter dash for those eight to ten. One's T-shirt virtually reached her knees. It didn't stop her, though, she came across first and the volunteer in her lane—a tight, dark, pretty girl, with a Mary Tyler Moore smile—hugged her and congratulated her. They both had astonishing spirit. And all the finishers behind were hugged also.

The high jump bar was placed at three foot two, and the path around it cleared. It sat, a straight crack in the world. Matt stepped off his ten steps and turned and found his starting spot. He rubbed his foot, making sure, like a batter in a batter box.

Trina coached him: "This is only three-two, Matt. You've done three-four. You can do this. Concentrate."

She stepped back, and he rocked forward and back once, looking at the ground, a hesitation, and then he went. He ran, gathering speed, and planted his left foot, and kicked up the right, scaled it, and over he sailed. Easily. He didn't stop in the pit, he was instantly up, right back to the exact spot, his spot. He never stopped now. Ten steps and turn and plant and dig and run and plant and kick and up and over. Three-four. Three-six. Up the field Mike had another dash. He could only look and try to see and root from a distance, and Matt cleared three-eight.

At the same time as Matt jumped, Tanana threw and cackled and rocked, and Sauros strode, and Dirty Raoul dribbled, and Waddles blocked that puck, and Carole Ann cheered, and Matt cleared three-ten, and Bruce ran.

He didn't win or come close. He started last and finished last, but he never slowed or stopped or gave up. He chugged. He raised his thumbs as he finished. "I'm Number One." That brought a cheer, so he raised his thumbs and said it again. Never had he had such an audience, and he took a bow.

Four-zero the bar said, and Matt missed his first attempt, and on his second the bar did a jig. It—*didn't* fall. He had cleared it. Trina felt gooseflesh on her thighs. He still hadn't stopped; she couldn't stop him or get him to rest. He just kept on going. His amount of effort took her breath away as well as his. She felt an exultation and also a kind of fear. She didn't want him killing himself, and she saw Mike and signalled him. He had an open moment.

The bar was moved to four-two, and Matt missed his first attempt, then missed his second. He dug in anew before his third, out of breath. He ran then and leaped. The bar *jigg-ig-gl-gled*. It held its purchase.

Mike reached them as the bar was set at four-four. Matt still didn't stop. He jumped and missed, and jumped and missed badly. Mike reached out and held onto him then.

"Take your time, catch your breath, don't hurry it, there's plenty of time," said Mike.

"Fosbury flop," said Matt, and pulled away.

He ran and turned his back to the bar and leaped and flopped. He did an actual Fosbury flop. He did it, only he missed and was out and didn't win.

Sauros fell in his two-hundred-meter heat. He was craning forward around a curve, and two others swung out and they all bumped. Only Sauros went down. He was so skinny and jagged, he was like a knife falling. He didn't stay down; he got to his feet. His knee and face were red. The scrapes bled as he tried to catch up.

"Come on, Sauros," Carole Ann cheered.

"Come on, Dinah," yelled Ransom. "Come on, Sauros."

Sauros took his huge, sharp, hook nose forward. He strained: for him effort was all, and he passed one, and two, and finished second. He was hugged, and then Mike embraced him.

"You did it, Dinosaur. You did it. You qualified for the final."

Higgenbottom long jumped. He looked especially good in his uniform, almost as sharp as he had in his tuxedo coat. He was a big fifteen-year-old, fair and handsome and muscular. His eyes were very pitted, though, and he could barely lift his feet. He had only three jumps, and his first one was six inches. He couldn't get off the ground even the length of his sneaker. It was a shock and pathetic at first. He tried extra hard on his second attempt. His arms swung as he had been taught, and his chin jutted. He made eight inches. Each extra inch then took on a great size; eighteen inches became a mile. There was a relationship between the infinite and the infinitesimal. Higgenbottom set for his third and final try. He swung his arms and swung them again. He let out a grunt as he leaped nine and a half inches. He had never jumped so far.

There was complete quiet before the blind races. Some games used beepers to lead the runners, but here it was started by gun and directed by verbal command. Volunteers ran backwards in front of the athletes urging them on. "Run. This way. This way. This way, Kevin."

Shirley Wazniak did a spin before her wheelchair race. She had only the use of two limbs, one foot and one arm. She had had to learn excruciatingly how to go in a straight direction. At the start she kicked her leg, pushed with it so she was traveling backwards. Her head spread back, her Adams apple jutted, and she turned one wheel cross-arm with her powerful, remaining forearm. It was a long, potent, wracking motion, but she finished. And there was pain in her glory, and glory in her pain.

The man next to Carl in the stands cried at Shirley's glory and her pain. He wore Madras pants and an alligator shirt and Weejuns. He and Carl had nothing in common, except the reason why they were here. Everything. Carl saw it, and he saw other families in the crowd and children and one or two pregnant women. There were many non-simple things on their faces. There were things even below the crying line. He put his arm around his daughter, and they watched Matt qualify for the four-hundred-meter final, wearing the visor cap Janice had put on him to protect him from the sun.

Some won and some did not. Some were good and some were not. Some strained and worked and others did not; they ran and jumped at a dignified pace. Many grinned as they finished, as they won, as they lost. It wasn't the outcome that counted.

Tanana threw a last ball, half-shotput, half-outfielder, and beat his chest like a bear. Jacey Bendel cruised to two-hundred-meter qualifying and final wins, her long hair flying and her eyes wild, a pretty, gifted athlete, as well as a t.m.r. Dirty Raoul dribbled and now he talked. Now he was Meadowlark Lemon, between the legs and around the back and little bounces with one knee down to the floor, with his special knee pad on, and if only he could shoot, too, but he couldn't, he was a lousy shot. Tom swam, and

Carole Ann cheered, and Sauros ran in his final. But despite his all, he only finished second.

"We now have with us, ladies and gentlemen," the announcer, Beverly Ziegenfuss, said, "two Hollywood stars who have come all the way from California to be with us today. Ron Masak and Pat Crowley! Let's hear our appreciation as Ron and Pat now present the awards for group two girls, two-hundred-meter run, group one boys two-hundred-meter run."

Ron Masak saluted the crowd and made a wisecrack, and Pat Crowley smiled. The winners came forward as their names were announced. Ron shook hands with each and Pat kissed each. The faces were a study: they smiled, they broke up, they were sober, they took it in stride, they raised V's.

Jacey received her gold medal, and her hair billowed forward as she leaned to have it hung around her neck. Sauros received his silver medal, and he stood at perfect attention until his name was called over the loudspeaker, and then his whole face broke open around his nose, the hugest grin. Silver medal on, he stepped back from Ron, face straight again, attention perfect again.

The relay came near the end of the day. Dirty Raoul ran the first leg and ran last, but made a perfect pass to Hunsucker. Hunsucker dug and got into third, and Sauros made it into second before he passed to Matt. They trailed, but not by too far.

Matt, still in his visor cap, was ready. He was off after first place, he was going to catch him. He ate up the yards. Up the inside he came, and then the boy in first place dropped his baton. It suddenly skidded out of his straining hand right into Matt's path. The boy stopped to retrieve it, and Matt started to roar by.

He had the race now, he had it—but he stopped. He picked up the other boy's baton for him and handed it back. The gesture cost him the race: third place zoomed by both of them, on the way to victory.

Mike shook his head, a mix of feelings, disgust, disbelief, and wonder finally at what his brother did do. Matt walked over to him, growing disconsolate, realizing defeat.

"You damn Samaritan," Mike said.

They began to walk, and he put his arm around his brother then.

In the stands Matt sat with his father and sister, waiting for the four-hundred finals, the last event of the day.

"How do you feel?" his father asked.

"I fine."

He was still drawing very deep breaths. Each had a slight wheeze as when he was asleep.

"You always say that."

"I do?"

"Yes, you do."

Matt struggled with his mind, and the limits of his vocabulary. "I fine and I—lucky."

"No, I lucky."

Carl wanted to say much: his child would always be mentally retarded—make no mistake—but Matt had changed. He had grown, he had learned, he had toughened, he had enjoyed. They all had, and Carl was proud. How could he tell his son? He wasn't sure he could, but he struggled with his mind and the limits of his taciturnity.

"You gave such a rip, Matt. That's what brought us here, together. Your grandmom wanted us to give you a moment, and you gave it to us. Such a son." And then he said, "You shook some iron."

"Shake more?" asked Matt.

"I don't know," his father said.

The volunteers gathered at one end of the stadium beneath the goalposts. The Red Cross leader got up on a ladder and spoke to the congregation:

"By the end of the four-hundred final these athletes, they're tired. They've given all. You have to keep them going and keep yourselves going," he said. "Always need fresh blood."

They booed him in mocking unison and broke, as from a huge huddle, and spread themselves around the entire track. They beaded its necklace and lined six deep its last seventy yards.

Mike loosened Matt up. He jogged with him, holding his hand.

"You loose?" he asked. "You ready?"

Matt nodded.

"You can do it . . . Star."

Matt said then, "I win this for you. I blow doors off."

The contestants lined up on the track along a staggered start. Matt was second from the outside. He dug in just as he did from his high jump spot. The gun went up and a runner jumped off, a false start. They lined up a second time, tense and expectant, and the gun rose and fired.

They were off, and nothing was going to stop Matt this time; his spirit was fierce, and he really moved, ignoring his tiredness, and Ransom and Cunningham cheered him, and Carole Ann, and Tanana and Sauros and Dirty Raoul and Waddles and Tom and Jim and Hunsucker and Higgenbottom, and Jacey, and even Bruce, cheered him. Carl found himself on his feet, everything in his throat, and he saw his running son, and his coaching son, and his daughter jumping up and down beside him, here, now, together. Carl cheered, and Mike cheered, and Matt shot by him, hugging the inside, and Mike cheered on from behind, but it was unsatisfactory, it wasn't enough, and he sprinted diagonally across the field so he could cheer on the opposite, final side. It was as fast as he had ever run, and Matt opened up a lead, he flew, and he soared around the final turn, only fifty yards from the finish, and he raised and spread his arms in salute of victory, in imitation of Mike, but he was premature. He had slowed, and with the tape only yards away, second place caught him, started to pass. But Matt realized it, and he wouldn't let him, and a last spurt, and

He just wouldn't let him pass.

THE BEST OF THE BESTSELLERS FROM WARNER BOOKS!

BLUE SKIES, NO CANDY by Gael Greene (81-368, $2.50)
"How in the world were they able to print **Blue Skies, No Candy** without some special paper that resists Fahrenheit 451? (That's the burning point of paper!) This sizzling sexual odyssey elevates Ms. Greene from her place at the head of the food-writing list into the Erica Jong pantheon of sexually liberated fictionalists."—**Liz Smith, New York Daily News**

DARE TO LOVE by Jennifer Wilde (82-258, $2.25)
Who dared to love Elena Lopez? Who was willing to risk reputation and wealth to win the Spanish dancer who was the scandal of Europe? Kings, princes, great composers and writers . . . the famous and wealthy men of the 19th century vied for her affection, fought duels for her.

THIS LOVING TORMENT by Valerie Sherwood (82-649, $2.25)
Perhaps she was too beautiful! Perhaps the brawling colonies would have been safer for a plainer girl, one more demure and less accomplished in language and manner. But Charity Woodstock was gloriously beautiful with pale gold hair and topaz eyes—and she was headed for trouble.

BLOOD OF THE BONDMASTER (82-385, $2.25)
by Richard Tresillian
Bolder and bigger than **The Bondmaster, Blood of the Bondmaster** continues the tempestuous epic of Roxborough plantation, where slaves are the prime crop and the harvest is passion and rage.

A Warner Communications Company

Please send me the books I have checked.

Enclose check or money order only, no cash please. Plus 35¢ per copy to cover postage and handling. N.Y. State residents add applicable sales tax.

Please allow 2 weeks for delivery.

WARNER BOOKS
P.O. Box 690
New York, N.Y. 10019

Name ....

Address ....

City .... State .... Zip ....

_____ Please send me your free mail order catalog

THE BEST OF THE BESTSELLERS FROM WARNER BOOKS!

I, CLEOPATRA by William Bostock (81-379, $2.50)
A big ancient-historical romance about history's first and foremost femme fatale. **I, Cleopatra** presents a striking new interpretation of the most famous sextress of all time: her own story as told by herself.

PASSION AND PROUD HEARTS (82-548, $2.25)
by Lydia Lancaster
The sweeping saga of three generations of a family born of a great love and torn by the hatred between North and South. The Beddoes family—three generations of Americans joined and divided by love and hate, principle and promise.

HOWARD HUGHES: THE HIDDEN YEARS (89-521, $1.95)
by James Phelan
The book of the year about the mystery man of the century—a startling eyewitness account by two of the aides who were closest to Hughes in his last secret years. "A compelling portrait . . . the best picture that we are likely to see."—**The New York Times Book Review**

MOSHE DAYAN: STORY OF MY LIFE AN AUTOBIOGRAPHY by Moshe Dayan (83-425, $2.95)
"A first-rate autobiography by a man who has been at the center of Israel's political and military life since before the rise of the state."—**Heritage**. 16 pages of photographs.

A Warner Communications Company

Please send me the books I have checked.

Enclose check or money order only, no cash please. Plus 35¢ per copy to cover postage and handling. N.Y. State residents add applicable sales tax.

Please allow 2 weeks for delivery.

WARNER BOOKS
P.O. Box 690
New York, N.Y. 10019

Name ....

Address ....

City .... State .... Zip ....

_____ Please send me your free mail order catalog